A CAT IN THE GHETTO

RACHMIL BRYKS

A Cat IN THE Ghetto

Stories by Rachmil Bryks

TRANSLATED FROM THE YIDDISH BY S. MORRIS ENGEL
WITH AN INTRODUCTION BY ADAM ROVNER
AFTERWORD BY BELLA BRYKS-KLEIN

A Karen & Michael Braziller Book
PERSEA BOOKS / NEW YORK

Persea Books
853 Broadway
New York, New York 10003

Library of Congress Cataloging-in-Publication Data
Bryks, Rachmil.
A cat in the ghetto : stories / by Rachmil Bryks; translated from the Yiddish by
S. Morris Engel; with an introduction by Adam Rovner—1st ed.
p. cm.
"A Karen and Michael Braziller Book."
ISBN 978-0-89255-327-3 (trade pbk. : alk. paper)
I. Engel, S. Morris, 1931- II. Title.
PJ5129.B7623C38 2008
839'.133—dc22
2007037599

Designed by Rita Lascaro
Manufactured in the United States of America
First Edition

Contents

INTRODUCTION

LONG BEFORE Holocaust literature courses became a staple on college campuses, writer and Holocaust survivor Yerachmil (Rachmil) Bryks struggled to relate the indescribable horrors he had witnessed to a younger and more fortunate generation. Though his memoiristic fiction caught the attention of such contemporary notables as Irving Howe and I. B. Singer, today his work remains mostly unknown. Bryks's relative obscurity is lamentable because he recognized and articulated the aesthetic and spiritual challenges posed by writing Holocaust literature. His intent, as he described it, was "to show to what Nazism can reduce man, yet also to reveal the spark of humanity in him." The stories collected in *A Cat in the Ghetto*, now thankfully back in print after many years, demonstrate his success. When these tales first appeared, their dark comedy and moral outrage likely alienated many. And Bryks's break with the subsequently well-established pieties of Holocaust literature is even more apparent today. Perhaps now, more than a half-century after they were first written, readers can come to recognize the urgency underlying these tales.

Rachmil Bryks was a budding Yiddish poet and actor prior to the outbreak of World War II. Following the Nazi invasion of Poland in 1939, he was interned in the Lodz ghetto, where he continued writing despite the misery of his circumstances. When the ghetto was liquidated in 1944, he was deported to Auschwitz and forced to abandon his manuscripts. Bryks was spared immediate death only to be pressed into the ranks of slave laborers in Germany. Years later, he recalled that he would lie on his bunk at night following exhausting days of toil and mentally rewrite his lost poems and prose. The U.S. Army liberated Bryks in 1945, and he then was brought by the Red Cross to Sweden to regain his shattered health. There he collected folkloric materials for the YIVO Institute of Jewish Research and began to chronicle his experiences of the *Khurbn*, as the Holocaust is termed in Yiddish. Several of the stories included in this collection were drafted during this period, and were later revised and serialized in the Yiddish press.

Like many survivors, Bryks made his way to New York and there rewrote and published the poetry he had originally composed in the ghetto. One of his shorter poems, "Do Not Despair," is included in this volume and provides a sense of his work's raw emotion. Readers of Yiddish will note that in the poem's manuscript form, the author's own hand records the year—1940—and place—the Lodz ghetto—of its composition. In New York, Bryks also oversaw the publication of his stories that depict Jewish life under Nazi rule, including later novels which remain untranslated. It is important to recall that Bryks wrote in Yiddish, the language of the majority of the victims of the *Khurbn*. In many ways, Yiddish remains the most appropriate language to record the murder, suffering, and heroism of millions. Yet since the devastation of Eastern European Jewry, few today speak, much less read, the language that defined a rich culture for centuries. The stories collected in this edition offer contemporary readers access to Bryks's empathic response to the *Khurbn*, in translations that preserve for English readers some of the folksy cadences of the Yiddish original.

Bryks may rightly be considered a folklorist of the *Khurbn* whose narratives are grounded in everyday details of speech, dress, and mannerism. As a number of critics have noted, including Irving Howe and Israeli scholar Dov Sadan, his work is primarily important as testimonial literature. The value of the stories gathered in this volume resides in the author's unflinching portrayal of the *Khurbn*, and his unexpected use of humor to depict the Jewish struggle for survival. Much of Bryks's writing reveals this amalgam of social observation, folkloric simplicity, and bitter irony. His wry documentary narratives thus serve as important links between the Jewish literature of dislocation produced prior to World War II, the later songs of ghetto performers and feuilletons of ghetto journalists, and the more stylized Yiddish fiction of the *Khurbn* by such authors as Chava Rosenfarb, Isaiah Spiegel, and Ka-Tzetnik (Yehiel [Feiner] De-Nur).

Like these writers, Bryks bears witness to the Nazi war against the Jews in both the ghettos and camps, and describes the contortions of body and soul he and millions of others endured. Although he uses fiction rather than memoir to transmute history into memory, Bryks avoids metaphor and imagery that might distance readers from the historical terror he records. His spare style is reminiscent of oral narrative, and by rejecting ornament and abstraction, his fiction offers an emotional directness that is often absent in works by contemporary writers who address the enormity of the *Khurbn*. As a result, his depiction of the Nazis and their victims is deeply disturbing for what it tells us about individual responsibility, and it is precisely for this reason that readers should hearken to Bryks's voice.

The attention Bryks pays to Jewish action under duress sets him apart from many other survivor writers, and likely also contributed to the lack of exposure his work has received. Bryks's fidelity to the past he bears witness to requires him to treat Jewish complicity in the form of *Kapos*, criminals, and members of the Jewish police and councils. As Hannah Arendt did in *Eichmann in Jerusalem*, and as Primo Levi did in his essay, "The Gray Zone," Bryks investigates how Jews were forced to cooperate in the hierarchy of their own annihilation. Unlike Arendt, Bryks pities the complicit, and he is much less reticent than Levi of passing judgment upon their actions. Nor was Bryks the only writer to rely on black humor to represent the absurd criminality of the Holocaust.

Polish writer and Auschwitz survivor Tadeusz Borowski conveys the casual brutality of industrial murder and the seemingly infinite capacity to accommodate horror in his mordant collection, *This Way for the Gas, Ladies and Gentlemen*. But Bryks differs from Borowski in that he does not use irony as a weapon to distort the humanity of his characters. Rather, irony becomes an instrument to evoke grief for his characters'—and our own— susceptibility to self-deception and dubious compromise.

Bryks paid special attention to the moral compromises made by the historical figure of Mordechai Chaim Rumkowski, the Nazi-appointed "Elder" of the Lodz Jewish council. Alternately considered a megalomaniacal collaborator or a tragic, misguided hero, he attempted to save a remnant of the Lodz ghetto through forced labor and compliance with Nazi demands for deportations. Rumkowski is mentioned in all of the stories in *A Cat in the Ghetto* and his policies form the backdrop for the conflicts that emerge. In "Kiddush Hashem," his collusion with the Nazis results in a frightening panorama of deportation, violence, and murder that culminates in Auschwitz. In the story "Berele in the Ghetto," he appears as a manipulative exploiter of child labor whose punitive tactics are foiled by the young hero who mocks him in song. Rumkowski's agents become the faceless adversaries who force a husband and wife to go to heartrending lengths to find cooking fuel for their ersatz meals in "A Cupboard in the Ghetto." But in the title novella, "A Cat in the Ghetto," the Elder's policies and the rumors and connivances they engender are treated with obvious black humor.

This acclaimed novella remains Bryks's most significant contribution to Holocaust literature. Generations of readers have been moved by this tragicomic tale of endurance that records the ghetto's poverty, hunger, and constant fear in an unadorned style. Bryks accomplishes this by drawing on comic characterizations familiar from folklore, and plot conventions reminiscent of the tales of *shtetl* hysteria found in the work of the Yiddish

INTRODUCTION

masters. And while the Yiddish literary greats whom Bryks
admired, including Sholem Aleichem, had utilized irony and
satire to confront the upheaval and violence faced by Jews in the
late 19th and early 20th century, Bryks writes with a black
humor that rejects the moral certainty of satire and the equa-
nimity of irony. Here Bryks attempts to sustain comic Yiddish
literary traditions ruptured by the *Khurbn*, traditions that successfully dealt with pogroms and war, but were seriously
strained by the attempt to cope with genocide.

In the novella "A Cat in the Ghetto," the ghetto residents'
Chelm-like capacity for fooling themselves reveals the author's
indebtedness to this tradition. The narrator describes the desper-
ate and absurd efforts to find sustenance: "Cabbage leaves and
radish leaves were the ingredients with which Jews prepared the
choicest dishes. . . . Having adopted the illusion that they were
eating meat—it was the flavor of meat they tasted. . . . Having
decided they were eating fish—it was the taste of fish they
savored." Elsewhere in the novella, humor repeatedly takes the
form of pathos mixed with irreverence. The narrator describes
the shortage of material to heat the ghetto's homes: "Many Jews
were consigned to crematoria over [the stealing of] a stick of
wood." At another point, a young boy complains that the potatoes in his portion of soup are rotten, exclaiming, "I thought I
was gassed they stank so bad!" And while the characters of the
novella do not appear to know about death camp gas chambers
or crematoria, the pitched irony for contemporary readers
results precisely from our consciousness of the historical Nazi
machinery of death. Macabre humor thus becomes a strategy
used to communicate vital truths about history and lived experi-
ence. The calculated sacrilege of the novella remains unsettling
even more than fifty years after its initial publication, but the
author's grim humor is important today precisely because it
upsets the decorum often observed in our memorializations of
the *Khurbn* and forces us to move beyond sentimental solace.

Moreover, Bryks insisted that his morbid ironies did not misrepresent the *Khurbn*. In a 1967 essay entitled "My Credo," which later appeared as an appendix to his untranslated novel *The Paper Crown* (1969), the author defends his use of the comic. Bryks notes that even "in the ghettos and the concentration camps there was humor and ridicule." He maintains that the existence of such gallows humor, and his duty as an eyewitness, actually require him to write with "humor and satire." Now, in a cultural moment that celebrates comic visions of the Holocaust, such as the fairy tale gloss of 1998's Oscar-winning *Life is Beautiful*, it is easy to forget that Bryks's humor is simultaneously faithful to history *and* destabilizing. In many ways, Bryks was ahead of his time, though interest in his work was reawakened a generation ago by American author Leslie Epstein, who lauded the power of his recollections. Epstein's award-winning novel from 1976, *King of the Jews*, evoked Bryks's fiction in its use of humor and in its focus on Rumkowski. Not surprisingly, both authors were taken to task for their approach and remain controversial today.

Bryks's original Yiddish 1952 edition, bound in burgundy leather and embossed with gold letters, rests on my bookshelf and has the sturdy, authoritative look of a prayer book. Yet for all its sanctity as testimony, the stories within feature few moments of redemption. And though the book's contents do not grant much comfort, Bryks's slim volume does provide a physical link to a literary tradition, a murdered culture, and the torments endured and recounted by one man. Persea's welcome reprint edition of *A Cat in the Ghetto* allows a new generation of English readers to hold Bryks's work in their hands, and see for themselves how the author's deceptively simple fiction reveals complex truths about men and women thrust into the abyss.

Adam Rovner,
University of Denver

My Credo

AN ESSAY BY RACHMIL BRYKS

Now, after a long time has passed since the publication of my books, *A Cat in the Ghetto*, *Kiddush Hashem*, "Berele in the Ghetto," *The Emperor in the Ghetto* and the rest, now after a whole literature has grown up round them, reviews, essays, appreciations, letters from readers and from writers, poets, artists, rabbis, Christian theologians, students, children— Jewish and non-Jewish, now after they have appeared in translation in several languages—European and Oriental, now after they have been the theme of college dissertations, of sermons and of public debates, I think I also have a right to say something about them, having come to realize that not everything that has been said and written about them is in accord with what I understood, and with my approach to the problem of how to write about the *Khurbn*, the Jewish Holocaust under the Nazis.

We must write about it in such a way that the world will know what happened, should not be allowed to forget what the Germans, aided by their creatures in other nations, did to the Jews and to others, to show to what Nazism can reduce man, yet also to reveal the spark of humanity in him. I want to emphasize that our *Khurbn* period includes also the spiritual *khurbn* in the Soviet Union during the Stalin era, the destruction of the Jewish word, the slaughter of Yiddish writers, actors, artists, teachers and others engaged in the field of Yiddish culture. They silenced our Yiddish and Hebrew speech. They made it impossible for those who wished to live and express themselves as Jews to do so.

How can this writing be done? By writing concisely, compressed, without embellishment, without adornment. We must not repeat. We must avoid any superfluous word in prose even more than in poetry. In poetry we can sometimes repeat a word or a whole line, to keep the rhythm. But never in prose.

A story must not have a superfluous episode, one that is not directly part of the narrative. I hold that the best-written reports of the *Khurbn* are Tuvia Borzykowski's *Tsvishn Falendike Vent* ("Between Collapsing Walls") and Leyb Rochman's *In Dayn Blut Zolstu Lebn* ("In Thy Blood Shalt Thou Live"). Both have the great merit of being real diaries, written at the time, in the midst of hell. And they have given us the maximum with a minimum of words. In poetry, the outstanding work is "The Song of The Murdered Jewish People" by Yitzhak Katzenelson, who himself perished in the slaughter. It is the Lamentations of the Third *Khurbn* in Jewish history. And the poems of the martyrs Mordecai Gebirtig, Hirsh Glick, Bunim Shayevitch and other anonymous poets who perished, who were "there" and wrote with great simplicity and with the Holy Spirit. That is why they have grown into the people, have become sanctified folk-poems. Those poems, on the other hand, that have not till now been adopted by the people will surely be lost and forgotten. Of the research literature into the *Khurbn* the most important works are those of Dr. Philip Friedman and Dr. Mark Dworzecki, because apart from their literary skill and style, they have the merit that these writers experienced the *Khurbn* themselves. We must also count among the best works the books that Professor Ber Mark wrote about the *Khurbn*.

We Jews have no tradition of creating large-scale novels. We wrote *megillot*, *aggadot*, and a chain of compact dramatic tales, stories and legends interwoven with chronicles, historical facts—one long tale, the Pentateuch and the rest.

It is only natural that I was influenced by the Russian and Polish classic writers and by our modern Yiddish literature, especially Abraham Reisen, David Edelstadt, H. Leivick and others. They made me think socially. I learned how to write from Mendele [S. Y. Abramovitsh] and Sholem Aleichem [Sholem Rabinovitch]. But I also learned how to write from the Bible. It was my greatest influence. The greatest influences in my writing *Oyf Kidesh HaShem* (*Kiddush HaShem*) were the *megillot*, the *midrash* and the Prophets. H. N. Bialik and Rawnitzky's *Di Yidishe Agodes* ("Book of Legends") and *Fun Gales Bevl biz Roym* ("From the Babylonian Exile to Rome,") by the Yiddish poet Bialystotzki also had a great effect on me. My *Oyf Kidesh HaShem* is a *megillah*. My "Berele in Geto" ("Berele in the Ghetto") is a *megillah*—a vale of tears of a Jewish child and his heroic spiritual and moral struggle against the tyranny of the Nazis.

In *Kats in Geto* (*A Cat in the Ghetto*) and *Der Keyser in Geto* ("The Emperor in the Ghetto"), I was also under the influence of the Bible and of Mendele and Sholem Aleichem. I mean with my humor and satire. But my humor and satire is more tragic, more bitter, more full of gall and wormwood, rending the heart, bringing tears.

Isaac Bashevis-Singer wrote: "*A Cat in the Ghetto* has a tragic humor unparalleled in world literature." Why? Because no other people and no other Jewish generation experienced such a catastrophe as our Jewish generation did in the Nazi ghettos and concentration camps—which I, by a thousand miracles, succeeded in surviving.

I feel that we must write about the Third *Khurbn* with humor, and I do so, because I saw that in the ghettos and the concentration camps there was humor and ridicule.

Jews always tried to divert the worst excesses against them with anecdotes. Against the enemy, their sole weapon was their mordant wit.

The ghetto produced hundreds of satirical jokes and anecdotes. Even the death camps did. One of the characters in my *Kiddush HaShem* said: "Here in Auschwitz we come in through the gate and we go out through the chimney." In *A Cat in the Ghetto,* Zabludovitch's wife exclaims: "I can hardly see your dimmed eyes. Believe me, Shloime, when I look at you I feel my flesh creep. What's to become of you? *Oy!* If only we had pull!" "Well, you know," Zabludovitch responds, "heads are superfluous in the ghetto: it's shoulders you need for pulling. . . . I heard a story of a woman who bore a child without hands, without feet, without a head. She wept bitterly, and the doctor consoled her: 'It's enough the child has shoulders; with pull he can get the best of everything!'"

This is folklore, reflecting life in those days. The *midrash*, and the *aggadah* are folklore with a moral. The Pentateuch, the entire Bible, the Talmud are woven through with folklore. All my stories are based on real facts, actual historical happenings interwoven with folklore.

Some want to know why I write so simply. I hold that we must express the most complex thought in the simplest way, so that everyone will understand. Those who can't write simply, as we talk, consider themselves modernists; they are abstract, like the modernist painters. But fashions come and fashions go. True literature abides. The modernists will always say: "The people are not advanced enough to understand us."

Another thing—I felt that when one writes about millions of people it weakens the tragedy. But if you tell the story of one individual, of one family, of one child, and you succeed in conveying their sufferings, their emotions, their state of mind, it gets across. But it must be written in such a way that the individual or the family or the child should symbolize the whole mass, the millions who were slaughtered.

It is not important to relate everything. One of the *Khurbn* writers has published a dozen books—and will no doubt publish more. Much of it is unimportant detail. A good deal is repetition. A writer more skilled in the art would have compressed his material into one or two really valuable books.

We must select the facts, sift them, and reveal what is general to them all, what sums it up. We must distill it as we distill brandy. Paint the way of life, the mode of dress, the ethnic quality, the language, the mentality. Create a fabula—what is to be the trunk of the tree, and what is to grow out of it, boughs and branches and leaves and fruit. It must be a tree, a complete growth, with all its parts, for it is tragic and horrifying. It must shake the reader, yet also hold him fascinated, so that he must read to the end.

I tried in my book, *Oyf Kidesh Hashem* (*Kiddush HaShem*) to picture Auschwitz in seventy pages. But I wrote the book over a period of six years, in pain and agony. In writing it I became a changed man. I didn't sleep night after night. I lived through everyone's separate torment. I experienced over again every happening I described. I was back in Auschwitz. When I did fall asleep I woke, screaming. I had dreamed I was in the ghetto or in Auschwitz.

I am reminded of the legend that Rabbi Amnon, when his hands and feet were cut off, composed in his death agony the "Unesaneh Tokef." Or that the *kol nidrei* prayer—words and music—were composed in the dungeons of the Inquisition. They are the expression of our feeling that the most valuable and most lasting works are created in pain and suffering. Only work created in suffering and pain has the power to shake people, body and soul, to stir their conscience, to refine and purify them and uplift them.

I concentrated on my task to reveal the essentially human element in man—to bring out the sparks of holiness in the Jewish soul, the Sabbath-sanctity of the Jewish woman, man and child. Their readiness to sacrifice themselves for others, for other people—which is greater than to sacrifice themselves for God—to redeem someone else's life at the cost of one's own. That is how Reb Aaron went to *kiddush hashem*—or rather to *kiddush*-Man, death in self-sacrifice not to G-d's Name, but Man's.

When the Germans ordered him to hand over ten Jews to be hanged, he refused, and himself went to the gallows. His daughter Dvora Leah, when they found a small Bible in Auschwitz, in order to save another woman said: "The Bible is mine!" She falls dead from a bullet fired into her by Dr. Mengele, one of the chief Nazi torturers in Auschwitz. Reb Aaron's granddaughter Rivkale offers to go voluntarily into the gas chamber to save other children—three generations immolated for the sanctity of human life.

Nor did I try to whitewash the Jewish renegades—the Jewish police, the informers, the *kapos*, the house-service, the *sonderkommando*, the members of the Jewish Council, the Party leaders, the traitors and the rest. I wanted to show what Nazism, what any form of dictatorship is capable of doing with a man, and how it does it. I also wanted to bring out the sense of trust, not losing hope, not losing one's faith in man, that in spite of everything, the world will be redeemed.

There are writers who were not "there," and even some who were there, who do all they can to obliterate and deny the truth. They are falsifying the catastrophe. They think that they are in this way giving greater sanctity to the *Khurbn*. They want to deny the inhuman acts committed by renegade and degenerate Jews against their own Jewish brothers and sisters. That is a crime. It is a desecration of their martyrdom. The Holy Torah did not shrink from telling us that when the Israelites were slaves in Egypt, the taskmasters set over them were also Israelites. The Torah did not hide anything. The Prophets did not keep silent about the iniquities committed by Jews against other Jews.

Art is not only aesthetic. Art is aesthetic and moral—especially Jewish art. We Jews have a way of asking—"*mai ko mashmo lon?*" or "What does it tell us?" We have no art for art's sake, because that does not tell us anything. A flower is not only lovely to the eye; it also has a pleasant smell. And it gives honey to the bee. The Greeks concentrated on beauty. We Jews always coupled beauty with morality. We always believed in *mussar* (ethics) and rebuke—in being told what is right and what is wrong. What we must not do. Our Prophets were great preachers of *mussar*. What can become of a man if he has not learned *mussar*?

All that I have discussed here was dictated to me by my intuition, while I was writing my books about the *Khurbn*, which I experienced myself. I had wanted to write only documents—in my own way—that would shock and shake the reader. Art does not interest me. Let those writers play about with it who write about the *Khurbn* without having been there. I fixed my aim when I first began to write about the *Khurbn*. If I have attained at least a part of what I have been discussing here, my work in carrying out my mission will not have been in vain.

Translated from the Yiddish by Joseph Leftwich

A CAT IN THE GHETTO

A CAT
in the
GHETTO

THE WAREHOUSES of the ghetto of Lodz were overrun by mice wreaking havoc with the food supplies stored there. To plant poison in the warehouses was out of the question because once the mice got hold of it, it could turn up anyplace—consequently there arose an urgent need for cats. But, alas, there were no cats in the ghetto. The Germans decreed that Jews were forbidden, on pain of death, to own any variety of domestic beast. Simultaneous with the sealing off of the ghetto, Jews had to deliver up all their animals to the *Kripo* (*Kriminal Polizei*), even dogs and cats. And because of the appalling hunger the cats ran away from the ghetto of their own accord. Besides, people ate cats. All of a sudden, a rumor spread through the ghetto: "Whoever turns in a cat—gets a two-kilo loaf of bread!"

No sooner did Jews get wind of this report than everyone's dream turned to catching a cat.

That's no trifle—a whole loaf of bread!

It happened on a fine summery evening, toward dusk. A few Jews were still working, putting in overtime at the dye works; in the watchman's shack sat Shloime Zabludovitch, twenty-four years old, engrossed in his reading. He was the factory watchman. A cannon could go off at his side—when Zabludovitch had his nose in a book he was as good as deaf. But when Mrs. Hershkowitz burst suddenly into the room calling out gleefully, "Mr. Zabludovitch, I caught a cat! We're partners. I'm sticking to our bargain: half a loaf for me and half for you!" Shloime Zabludovitch forgot momentarily about his book.

That's no small change—half a loaf!

"Really!?" The word shot out of him with as much force as if he had just discovered the war was over.

Without a moment's delay, Mrs. Hershkowitz brought in the cat, saying: "You see? When God is ready, He lends a hand."

Zabludovitch could feel his heart swell with joy. He was afraid to lay a hand on the cat. Never in all his days had he held a cat in his arms.

Let her loose? She might, God forbid, take off. So he blurted out as if a brilliant idea had struck him: "You know what, Mrs. Hershkowitz? Bring me a sack and we'll put the cat in!"

The good woman brought in ticking from a featherbed (which the Germans used to toss in the bloodied clothing of the Jews they murdered, to be dyed; Jews then were forced to weave them into rugs for the Germans). It was not the easiest thing in the world for Zabludovitch to prod the cat into the sack. They both tied her in. He folded up the ticking and placed it carefully on the bench. Since the ticking was long enough to cover a mattress, the cat was able to lower herself to the floor. She crawled across the entire length and breadth of the ticking, complaining plaintively "meow, meow, meow!" as she searched for a way out.

Mrs. Hershkowitz was a broken reed of a woman, a widow. At home her orphaned brood cried and yammered for something to eat. She stood in line at the kitchen for soup, and at the cooperative for her ration. There was not a minute's time to spare and she was in a hurry to get home. So she said: "My dear Mr. Zabludovitch, you have plenty of time; I'm sure you won't cheat me. Here's the cat, I leave her in your hands. First thing tomorrow morning take her to the food distribution agency, pick up the bread, and we'll divide it between us."

Zabludovitch assured her that she could rely on him, she said good-night, and left for home.

These days one doesn't share a piece of bread even with one's own mother—that's the ghetto. . . . Then why did she take him on as a partner? Because they both had responsible jobs: he searched the men, she, the women, to make sure that no one was stealing anything from the factory on the way out. Both managed to look the other way from time to time, to keep from endangering the lives of the workers. Linked by these secrets, they were at all times prepared to help each other, and in the course of conversation, they once exchanged a solemn promise that if either one should corner a cat, they would share the proceeds as equal partners.

A washerwoman came in from the courtyard carrying two empty pails for water. Zabludovitch always let her have hot water from the dye works. "My dear Mr. Zabludovitch," she demanded, hearing the cat meowing, "is that a cat you have?" She sounded like someone asking whether he'd won a million. "I guess congratulations are in order. *Mazel tov!*—you'll be getting a whole bread! Yes . . . and a hundred marks too! Do you happen to know the price of a loaf of bread these days? Ask me—I know it! A loaf of bread comes to one thousand eight hundred marks! That's the way it is, my dear sir! Rumkowski's republic has certainly come a long way (Rumkowski was the head of the ghetto of Lodz). On the card, eighty pfennig a loaf; on the street—a thousand eight hundred marks! Let me have the cat—I have pull at the administration. There's just one thing—I want half a loaf of the bread!"

Zabludovitch replied that unfortunately the cat was not his alone to give since he was already pledged to a partner.

"In that case, Mr. Zabludovitch," she responded at once, "you can each give me a quarter of a loaf. Better still, I'll let you have right this minute a quarter of the loaf which I just got today, if you give me the cat. It's already too late now, they're closed for the day, but first thing tomorrow morning I'll dash over to the food administration building and bring you a whole loaf of bread and a hundred marks to boot, maybe more! I know the right wires to pull—I do the big boss's laundry—so you can be sure you'll get the rest, but for that I want a half a bread right now."

Zabludovitch thought it over carefully: an opportunity like this is not to be handed lightly over to someone else. True, he has no pull, but when he walks into the building, the cat will prove to be his best source of influence. I can't trust the cat to any-one—suppose she takes the bread and I'm left with nothing! Am I going to complain to the *Judenrat*!?

"No!" he answered resolutely.

The woman refused to retreat. Nothing short of getting the bit of bread would do, and she became more and more insistent, endlessly importuning and coaxing. By then she had forgotten what brought her there, and kept wheedling him to accept the half-kilo of bread.

Zabludovitch was terribly hungry. Since he had come to the ghetto this gnawing hunger had never been appeased. And so he said: "All right, bring your quarter of a loaf—but make sure it's an honest weight! Then you can take the cat and tomorrow you'll add the rest. That way you'll get a whole half a loaf for yourself, and my partner and I will also only have half a loaf."

"Fine," the woman replied, satisfied at last, "I'll bring it right away," and went out. Back in her own house she reflected. Bread rations are precious, more valuable than diamonds! Should I hand out my ration in advance when the bread I just received has to last me for eight days? And me without a thing to cook? No, I'm not going to give it to him.

Pangs of hunger became stronger and more frequent, overwhelming Zabludovitch. He was sure that any minute now the washerwoman would be returning with the bread. She did not come back.

All the while the cat hadn't left off her plaintive meowing. She kept shifting, shuffling along the length and breadth of the ticking sack. She was groping for a way to free herself.

Old Lande here is the boilerman. Begrimed, like a chimneysweep, small, skinny, shrunken, he is as withered as a dried mushroom. He is an ex-restauranteur. His place of business used to be situated in one of the most beautiful spots in Lodz— on Petrikov Street.

He is known as a glutton. Not because he eats so much, but because he talks so much about eating: what he would eat if he could, and what he did eat before the war, giving a detailed accounting of his meals from Sunday to Sunday—his favorite breakfast dishes, his favorite dishes for the evening meal and for a late snack at night; everything he used to eat at his country place on the farm and all the drinks he particularly enjoys. He enumerates the various cognacs, champagnes, whiskies, blended liquors—both strong and weak. When he speaks, it is obvious that he is savoring the taste of the dish. One could literally see his mouth water.

As soon as he got wind of the discovery of the cat, he made straight for the watchman's shack in a single breath, his pipe stuffed full of cherry leaves and still clenched between his teeth. As usual, he was seized with a fit of coughing and stammered. "M-m-m Mister Zabludovitch, *mazel tov*! I hear congratulations are in order! So you found a cat! How fortunate you are.... When a man has luck on his side, there's nothing more to be said.... About a year ago I almost had a lucky break too."

Taking the pipe in his hand, he continued with a smug little smile:

"I almost caught a cat then. She slipped out from under my very hand and escaped! I won't lie to you, I wasn't the only one involved—I had a few partners. Where do you suppose can this cat have come from? She must have come from town. Sneaked in through the barbed wire. Completely fooled the ghetto guards. She must belong to an enlisted man or maybe to some personage even higher up. These days it's not just any German that owns a cat. You know they gorge themselves on roast cat. Ooh, does that taste good; I could wish myself a year that good. Cat's pretty juicy and fat, but you have to wash it down with a slug of whisky, then another, and another. And then prolong the whole thing with a cigarette, properly, not with this rubbish!" pointing to his pipe. "Woe is me! I've already one foot in the grave; I mean, I'm sinking fast! Wherever I look, everything's a blur and my head's whirling round like a carrousel. I managed to shove down four soups today, upon my life, and yours too! It's plain water. . . . I felt worse after the soup than before. If only I could lay my hands on some potato skins! I don't suppose you happen to know a kitchen where they cooked potatoes today? . . . Yes, well, to get back to what I was about to tell you, how close I came to striking it lucky too. A year ago, when I was in Marishin (a suburb in the ghetto where workers who had influence were allowed to spend two weeks), taking the rest cure, we were sitting outdoors at dusk. That's the time of day cats always go meandering around. We just happened to catch sight of it: over the barbed wire, a cat was slowly making her way. We were all praying for her just to crawl over into the ghetto. We worked out a plan on how to capture her. You may be sure, my dear Mr. Zabludovitch, if that cat had crawled into the ghetto—she would've been mine! My name isn't Lande for nothing, you see, and I'm the one with real pull at the food administration! She was right at the wires when the German, curse him, chased her back, may he drop dead where he stands. At the food administration I have real pull. All these crooks, you see, used to gorge themselves and swill liquor at my place. I had some restaurant in those days, roast gizzard, and stuffed neck, and chopped livers, and. . . . What's the use, am I going to give you a complete account of every menu? Take my advice, dear sir, and make me your partner! Let me have the cat, I'll get the bread, and we can share it—I guarantee it, I'll pledge you something very valuable—or may I sicken over every bite I deprive you of! On the word of Lande!"

But Shloime Zabludovitch replied steadfastly, "No, I don't need a partner."

"What's that, Mr. Zabludovitch? What do you mean? When you get right down to it the cat belongs to all of us here at the factory. Now, where was the cat caught? In the factory, eh? She should belong to all of us! We should all be partners equally; we should all go together to the administration with the cat, take the bread, and divide it amongst us all! Because today no one can be entrusted with bread! This is a ghetto, understand? But, of course, since you are after all Zabludovitch, I do not begrudge you the joy of it from the bottom of my heart, you are welcome to the whole thing."

He added this last at the end to curry favor with Zabludovitch; after all, he was the one who searched him as he left the factory. . . .

Night fell. The night watchman arrived—a tall big-boned *yekke*, a German Jew, whose grandfather had himself baptized, and so he, the grandson, was shipped off to the Lodz ghetto. When he detected the sound of the cat meowing, he grew cheerful and remarked with a smile:

"*Herr* Zabludovitch, *sie haben eine Katze? Verkaufen sie mir! Sie bekommen fünfzig Mark, ich werde am Abend machen ein Katzenbraten!*" (Mr. Zabludovitch, you have a cat? Sell her to me! You'll get fifty marks, and in the evening I'll make a cat roast!)

"Butcher the cat? Never—not on your life! Not even for two loaves of bread! What in the world—roast cat! It's obvious you're no Jew!"

"Zicher bin ich kein Jude! Ich bin Reichdeutsche. Mein Grossvater ist Jude gewesen! Ich bin Reichsdeutsche! Und die dumme Nazis haben mich eingesiedelt in ghetto! Donnerwetter!" (Certainly I'm no Jew! I'm a German national. My grandfather was a Jew! I'm a German national! And the stupid Nazis put me in the ghetto. Confound it!) Here he lowered his voice, and enlightened him in German mixed with a little Yiddish. He delivered a whole scientific lecture on the *calorie* content of meat as compared with the *vitamin* content of bread—concluding with emphasis on the greater value of meat. "You are all swollen up, your bones suffer from calcium deficiency, and so you must eat meat . . . You'll get from me half a roasted cat. This half a cat will make you healthy; cat is very tasty, and cat is very clean. My legs are also swollen. Half a cat will make me well, too. *Calories, calories!* They are of the utmost importance for the body's well-being!"

Zabludovitch was beginning to feel nauseated and shouted at him: "It's easy to see you're no Jew! I'd vomit at such a meal!"

After lengthy deliberation, Zabludovitch carried the cat into the dye works. He set her down in a corner on a heap of bloodied rags, and left for home.

On the empty plots of ground between the crowded buildings, on bits of soil which the sun never reached, Jews planted gardens. Soil?—it was composed of coaldust, bits of broken bricks, stones, glass—soil such as could never have thirsted to become fruitful. . . .

Still—Jews put such pains and drudging toil into their gardening, that here and there a few lettuce leaves somehow managed to push their way up, a few scattered bean plants so sparse that the stems could be counted on one hand. . . . Jews dug up the cobblestone pavement to get at a bit of earth. Some of them even strewed earth over the pavement.

Of all the seeds, radishes were the easiest and most plentiful crop. So they sowed radish, and the earth produced only a few anemic looking radish leaves. And so they took to eating radish leaves.

All over the world leaves are green; here, they were white, and whoever had the tiniest scrap of earth planted radish: on sidewalks, in a box, in meat cans, in the baby carriages that remained after the "Curfew" (the "Curfew" was the period of the great "selection," lasting seven days and seven nights—in the year one thousand nine hundred forty-two—which was the year the Germans took away nearly all the old folk and children—altogether twenty-two thousand persons). Yes, baby carriages were left over, and Jews poured soil into them and planted radishes. Radishes were planted in window boxes as well, and in a few weeks the lucky owner had radish leaves which, when cut down, gave way to new growth of radish leaves in a few days.

Cabbage was also seeded, because huge, wild leaves also sprouted from the plants. Cabbage leaves and radish leaves were the ingredients with which Jews prepared the choicest dishes: a variety of soups, spinach, salads, pancakes, even fish and meat.

How could they possibly have made meat? They chopped up the cabbage or radish leaves, sprinkled it with some salt and ersatz paprika, and fried it. Water had to be added to the pan, drop by drop, to keep the food from burning, since shortening of any kind was unavailable. Having adopted the illusion that they were eating meat—it was the flavor of meat they tasted.

How, again, did Jews prepare fish? They chopped up the cabbage or radish leaves, sprinkled it with some salt and ersatz paprika, then they added a couple of saccharin pills, and cooked it. A few saccharins were also tossed into the broth. Having decided they were eating fish—it was the taste of fish they savored. Unremitting hunger caused their palates to atrophy so that they couldn't distinguish between one flavor and another.

Overnight, hands, feet, face, belly swelled up. People weren't able to move and remained immobile, lying on their filthy mattresses. If after a great expenditure of energy and effort they finally succeeded in bringing a doctor round, the doctor would take one look at the patient and shout: "Stop eating cabbage leaves! Stop eating radish leaves! They only make you swell up!"

And the Jews replied lamenting, "Then give us bread! Give us potatoes! Or something else to eat! Doctor, sir, what should we eat? Hunger keeps plaguing us...."

The sick, lying on their mattresses, became skinny and emaciated, thin as rails, leaving only marrowless, parched bones, with dead skin drawn tightly over them and limbs running with pus. They lay thus awaiting the approach of their redeemer: death.

Some were redeemed sooner; the abdomen burst like a pricked balloon, the water gushed out, and they were spared prolonged suffering.

Very often such an individual was removed to the hospital. German doctors arrived from outside the ghetto and experimented on him as if he were a laboratory mouse until he died in their hands.

But not everyone owned his own radish leaves or cabbage leaves. The greater number of people had to buy them, and since money was worthless, the currency was bread. Once the leaves were obtained, there was still the problem of getting them cooked. Rations for wood and coal were nonexistent, and people put their lives in jeopardy for fuel. Many Jews were consigned to crematoria over a stick of wood. They tore down dressers, fences, took apart whole houses. They stripped away the moldings from the doors and windows of their own homes, ripped up the floors, burned all the furniture, so long as it was wood. Every week the building managers accompanied by police made inspection rounds, house after house, in an attempt at control, but it was useless. Jews risked their lives to have the wherewithal to cook their bits of cabbage and radish leaves.

* * *

It is time to return to Zabludovitch. Opposite his window on the courtyard, Zabludovitch sprinkled sand on the pavement and made his own "garden," the whole thing about four meters long. He had actually sprinkled sand for a larger plot, but his neighbors envied and resented it and took some away. "How come?" they clamored, "You're taking all this for yourself? Wouldn't you like to grab the whole earth for yourself?"

Working his plot of ground made Zabludovitch ill. He ached in every joint. He could neither stand upright, nor walk, nor lie down. He predicted his own imminent death. But a neighbor massaged his whole body with wood alcohol he had through some miracle procured and after a few days of bedrest he recovered.

Zabludovitch had planted his seeds densely, utilizing every grain of sand to the utmost: behind the cabbage he first planted a bit of radish, behind the radish, a beet, behind the beet, a carrot, behind the carrot, a parsley root, behind the parsley, he smuggled in a radish once more. And the plants began to behave like modern states—they fought among themselves for so long that they completely destroyed one another.

The cabbage leaves began to grow wild. Each leaf took up a whole meter in length. Zabludovitch's heart swelled with pride, expanding with the cabbages. He conjured up fantastic images of the dishes he would prepare when the cabbage was ready—a dish of genuine meat and fish.

He ate up the cabbage leaves, bitter as gall, with great relish; but at the spot where the actual head of cabbage was supposed to have grown, worms had unfortunately slipped in.

In the beginning, he believed birds were eating up his cabbage because little round holes appeared, as if the birds had pecked at it, but on closer examination he noticed that the undersides of the leaves seemed to have been dotted as though with a rainfall of tiny worms invisible to the naked eye and the same color as the leaves. Suddenly, in the course of a single night, only skeletal remains were left of the plantings, all uniformly blanketed in green, snakelike worms with stripes of brown, gold, and black. Zabludovitch had an idea: he sprayed the plants with lime, but to no avail. He sighed mournfully. "Hard luck! What can you do? If you're meant to starve—that's it!" *Resignation*

Zabludovitch had better luck with the radish; besides the radish leaves, a little radish also sprouted. As soon as he picked the radish, he immediately strewed some new radish seed into the same scooped-out little hole in the seedbed. Thus he was able to make use of the soil three times through the summer. (Later on he planted only radish quite densely, to be sure of having a great many radish leaves in the future.) He sprinkled plenty of salt over the radish, added the bit of rationed synthetic bread made of corn and chestnut flour, and drank it down with a pot of boiling hot colored water bought in the kitchen of a coffee-house, for who dared permit himself the luxury—the debauchery—of building a fire at home? For him, this was a feast.

Zabludovitch lived in a raised one-story house: underneath, taking up the whole length of the house, stretched the cellars. During the summer, the cellars were flooded with water standing a meter deep, and in winter there was more than a meter of ice. The little house was always damp.

Summers it was possible to cool off by stretching out on the floor; winters, the house appeared to have been built of ice: the ceiling, the walls, and the floor were all iced over.

During the summer the walls became black and crumbled. Zabludovitch had built himself a little stove of bricks, tin, and a tin pipe, and set it up in a corner near the door. In a second corner stood a clothes rack on which hung the few pieces of old clothes. One wall was overloaded with Jewish books that he had brought into the ghetto with him, gathered from the homes of the Jews who had been deported.

In another corner stood his valise. He kept his little store of food there. In the middle of the room, atop a four-cornered pile of bricks, lay a heavy sheet of iron covered over by a threadbare old tablecloth. This was the table. Nearby lay small mounds of bricks that served as chairs.

The two sacks of straw lay on the bare clay that had once been part of the torn-up floor. The windowsill was also ripped out. The fragments of woodwork had all been devoured by the stove long ago to cook up a meal.

Right now his wife, Hannele, was standing in the dark and by the light of the moon she threw the last spindly chips of wood from the last drawer of all that was left her of the cabinet in which she kept the linens. She had just cooked some radish-leaf soup and was frying meat made of cabbage leaves.

She also prepared a new dish—a sweet stew made of coffee grounds that the Jews in the ghetto referred to as coffee-grime, composed of burnt-barley grain and chaff from which the Germans had previously extracted the flour by chemical means. Each head of household received about a half kilo every fifteenth day. The price—a day's wages. The Jews ate it from the sack with spoons. It set the bowels on fire.

Hannele brought home a recipe she got at the factory: taking some of the coffee mixture she sprinkled it into a utensil and poured a bit of warm water over it, added a few drops of oil, a few saccharin tablets, a teaspoon of sugar—and created a sweet confection.

As soon as Zabludovitch stepped into the house he began to relate the story of the great good fortune he encountered that day: he had a cat!

"Tomorrow, Hannele, we'll eat bread until we're full!"

They finished up the bit of watery radish-leaf soup and cabbage-leaf meat by moonlight. She cautioned him not to eat the bread he was going to get for the cat all at one sitting, but to divide it up into portions for two-three days.

"You're swelled up so much already," she said, "I can hardly see your dimmed eyes. Believe me, Shloime, when I look at you I feel my flesh creep! What's to become of you? *Oy*! If only we had pull!"

"Well, you know," Zabludovitch tried to joke, "heads are superfluous in the ghetto: it's shoulders you need for pulling . . . I heard a story of a woman who bore a child without hands, without feet, without a head. She wept bitterly, and the doctor consoled her: "It's enough the child has shoulders; with pull he can get the best of everything!"

"That's how it is, Shloime, I, who speak four languages and supervised all the correspondence in the largest office in Lodz, I'm only a two-legged horse dragging a wagon . . ."

"Every time I see you," Zabludovitch said, "my heart aches! Where is your plump round face? We're not even twenty-five, neither of us, and we look like death's-heads. On the other hand—the war might be over any minute now! And the most important thing is: tomorrow, Hannele, we eat until we're stuffed! Bread!"

Needing to comfort him in turn, she regaled him with some coffee-grime. He finished it off as though it were a chunk of chocolate, feeling more drained than ever when he was through.

He continued aloud to console himself:

"Tomorrow we eat until we're satisfied."

Hannele sliced off a few extra pieces of the next day's portion of bread, charging it to tomorrow's windfall. They finished eating and lay down to sleep as contented as they had been on their honeymoon.

Zabludovitch had a dream that night: he is walking into the administration building carrying the cat, when he sees a supply-room full of sacks: flour, sugar, beans, grain, and bread, layer upon layer, from floor to ceiling. The boss, Herr Shtchenshlivi, plump and well nourished, with a fat red neck, stands behind the counter. Raising his eyes abruptly, he glares out from under his glasses. When he catches sight of the cat, his round moon-face dissolves into a tiny smile that flows around his whole face.

Happily Shtchenshlivi grabs the cat from Zabludovitch—and hands over a loaf of bread. Zabludovitch breaks off a piece on the spot and eats it. Perceiving this, "Are you that hungry?" Herr Shtchenshlivi inquires. So saying, he hands him another loaf. In one breath, Zabludovitch runs home to his wife, holding both breads clutched tightly in his arms in mortal fear that they might, God forbid, be snatched away from him. He wants to get home as quickly as possible. He runs and runs. He is actually rising up into the air. Until—he drops down onto the floor of his house. When he woke up with a start, he found himself in bed.

In the morning, as his wife was dressing to go to the factory, Zabludovitch said to her, "Hannele, today's the day we get bread. I had an absolutely marvelous dream. Shtchenshlivi himself, the one who devours us alive, he took the cat from me himself and gave me not one, but two loaves of bread! You do believe in dreams, don't you, eh Hannele?"

She gazed at him reflectively and saw how much he had swelled up overnight, and how pouches had formed under his eyes. With a deep sigh, she intoned: "Father in heaven! Let me live to see the day that I can serve a whole loaf of bread on my table and we can just slice from it as much as we want to."

"Wait and see, Hannele," he comforted her, "today we'll eat bread until we're full."

She wished him luck and left for work. Outside, she was overcome with pity, and opening the door again she said: "Shloime, have a piece of my share of the bread, too."

Shloime Zabludovitch worked the second shift: from two in the afternoon to ten in the evening, so he could have allowed himself the luxury of sleeping a little longer. But he was too restless to lie in bed. As soon as his wife had gone, he dressed and went across the road to "Tier-Zucht"—a stable where the cows, goats, sheep, and hens were kept that provided milk and eggs for the *Judenrat*. Fresh vegetables were sent here from the greenhouses: carrots, beets, potatoes, pea pods, kohlrabi, and cauliflower. This was feed for the animals.

Zabludovitch was a frequent visitor here. He used to bring the boss and the workers reports of the news he heard on the underground radio. And once in a while, he would receive in return some vegetables in summer, and in winter—some scrapings of potato peel or kohlrabi sent from the kitchens. From all this, he had set up a *cholent*.

Since they had no fuel for a fire, the Jews hit on a scheme for making *cholent*. The baker's oven retained heat for twenty-four hours. When the last breads were shoved out, *cholents* were shoved in, cooked in four hours, and the process was repeated again and again. Later on, special *cholent* bakeries were established where *cholent* made up of radish leaves, cabbage leaves, and a variety of scrapings was baked three-four times daily. And so Zabludovitch went in here to share the good news.

No sooner did the boss discover that Zabludovitch had a cat, than, "Just bring me the cat," he said. "Of course you know that I have pull at the food administration, but you've got to give me half a loaf of bread for my trouble. After all, if a total stranger would get one bread, I would certainly get two. Go ahead and get the cat, don't dawdle. Time is precious! Better still, I'll buy the cat from you for an egg; you obtain a big, beautiful, fresh egg in exchange for the cat! What do you say to that?"

In the ghetto they had already forgotten what an egg looked like.

When Zabludovitch left, the watchman sidled up to him on all fours. He was known as Klepsidre—"obituary"—because he looked like a corpse. Although it was the Tammuz season and very warm, hunger made him shiver as though with cold. He was bloodless, and his nose was constantly dripping. He crawled on all fours like a baby—on the ground or against the walls. He was not yet thirty. Lice feasted on his body, and the mud and filth finished off his clothes: his shoes had long been lacking soles.

This watchman, David Klepsidre, murmured into Zabludovitch's ear: "You'll get half a kilo of bread from me straightaway! I'm going to get it this minute! Here, see my card! Do you see the number?"—shoving the card up before his eyes. "I'm the one with real pull at the administration! Bring me the cat! I have a wife and two little ones. It breaks my heart to see them so swollen, overnight! Who can tell if it's from the radish leaves or just from not eating, but a small piece of bread might save their lives! I need the bread more than the boss—he can take care of himself. Remember, the cat belongs to me! Do you hear me?"

Zabludovitch considered: "It's really a pity about Klepsidre's children, but am I any less swollen? What does my wife always say?—'If you had a bread as big as your swollen face, the swelling would go down.'... They must think they're dealing with some idiot. As if I'm going to spoon-feed them—put the bread right in their mouths! For goodness sake, can't I find my own way to the food administration building? I own the cat! When I get the bread I'll give his children a few pieces of it myself."

With this comforting thought he went home. He pulled on his coat and dragged himself off to the factory.

Shloime Zabludovitch had a long way to go. While he was walking, shuffling along on his swollen feet, he spent the time thinking over everything that had happened. Trucks passed him by, packed to the top with finished merchandise from the tailor shops: military uniforms and civilian clothing. With each truck rode a ghetto official wearing a pale yellow band on his left arm and a Jewish policeman in civilian clothes, wearing shiny boots and a round little khaki cap with an orange band two centimeters wide, with a bar in the center. On his left arm, a pale yellow band with a dark blue star of David. On the star of David—a metal number, and in his hand—a bludgeon. They guarded the merchandise.

Farther on stretched a long train of carts of manure, barrels of fecal sewage, drawn by fathers, mothers, grandmothers, grandfathers, children. . . . The carts and barrels were hung with pots from which the two-legged horses ate their soup rations. The leaking barrels left a trail along the entire way. The older children sat on top of the barrels, and the suckling babies lay in the wagons. Children followed their mothers hanging onto their skirts. Some mothers held onto a child with one hand, and pushed a barrel with the other.

Faces, hands, and feet were splattered with feces. Their clothing—tattered rags—was soaked in manure. They wore heavy wooden shoes. Their feet wrapped in rags. Half naked. Their flesh—dehydrated mushrooms, without essence, shadows, the width of late-spring mayflies. . . . The Tammuz midsummer sun heated the metal barrels, and the manure boiled. The stench made it difficult to draw a deep breath.

Now and then, the dense atmosphere was pierced by bursts of coughing from the diseased lungs of the "fecalists."

The overfed boss of the wagon train is on the sidewalk—he has the concession from the Germans. He spurs on his two-legged horses with deafening curses that resound through the streets: "Faster! Faster!"

It now happened that Shloime Zabludovitch had to pass the ghetto fence, made of boards and barbed wire. Helmeted soldiers had been dawdling around the fence all week, dressed in green and khaki uniforms and carrying guns with spears that gleamed in the sun. Zabludovitch shuffled along stealthily, in deadly fear lest the soldiers decide to amuse themselves by using him for target practice as they so often did.

High up in the air overhead, heavy bombers were cruising around. Soldiers were marching through the gate in the fence singing, "On to England! Tomorrow the whole world belongs to us!—*Deutschland, Deutschland, über alles!*"

Artillery shots echoed from the nearby woods, where soldiers were training. Along the road, peasants from the villages rode by on their wagons loaded with vegetables, fruits, and poultry, a sight that intensified his hunger.

Then he came to Rumkowski's winter palace. From his side of the tall fence he could only catch a glimpse of the roof and a bit of red brick wall. He gazed thoughtfully at the field, observing the growth of potatoes, beets, carrots, onions, garlic. There was only wire fencing around the field. And policemen stood guard to prevent any starveling from stealing. Farther down, he could see a meadow of close-cropped green grass, a few score meters in length. A fat cow stood in the middle tied to a post. A goat and her kids were grazing and now and then the kids hopped up to the low-hanging branches of the young saplings and chewed off new leaves. The livestock belonged to the head of the ghetto— Mordecai Chaim Rumkowski.

Living corpses lay in the meadow, faces like dried-up dead grass. . . . They were trying to tear up the grass and put it to their mouths. The shepherd, a Jew, holding a long shepherd's crook in his right hand, with a yellow band on his left arm, and his left breast and right shoulder stained by yellow patches the shape of a Star of David, chased them off, yelling:

"Are you trying to get me sent away out of the ghetto to a camp on account of you? I'm responsible for these animals getting enough to eat!"

Zabludovitch kept reminding himself of his good fortune in having a cat. . . . Today was the day he would eat his full. . . .

Now he was approaching the window of a "zashilkovietz," one who lived on relief. During this period a number of the ghetto inhabitants were on relief, receiving from the *Judenrat* seven marks a month, a sum certainly not enough to live on. But this suited the Germans well. They said: "These paupers are not productive, so they must be deported." And, indeed, they were the first to fall victim to the gas chambers and crematoria. . . . The seven marks couldn't be stretched to cover even the rations. Such a person traded with his life: he sold his bread, and had enough to buy rations. Then he sold his rations—and bought coffee-grime and watery soup from the kitchen, on his card. He also bought some *Irisen*, nicknamed, "an hour on the tongue," produced in the ghetto from sugar that the employees sneaked out of the cooperatives. The *Irisen* were diluted with sand and they stayed in the mouth for a while.

Children on the street intoned with mournful voices, "*Irisen*! *Irisen*! Big chunks! An hour on the tongue! Two marks a piece! A prescription for surviving the war!" Jews gnawed on these sand-coated confections and drank water until they swelled up and fell into their beds. Thus "zashilkovtzes" turned into "klepsidres".

Zabludovitch had now arrived at the place of business of one such "zashilkovietz." A large display window stood out here—one in a million! Inside the window lay a complete ration, newly purchased. Volunteer buyers were not wanting. It was, in fact, a miracle that the Almighty created "zashilkovtzes"—or else, heaven forbid, the "beiratovtzes" (those privileged persons who received special allotments) and the higher-up ghetto officials might also have turned into "klepsidres."

Flies peppered the panes and the boards were well-salted. Spiders adorned the far corners of the window with woven cob-webs that reflected the sun in rainbow colors. The wall was scaling and crumbled. On the board, the wares were laid out—an entire allotment for fifteen days: a piece of bread, raw, baking in the sun; a little cup of flour; a cup of wormy peas; a teaspoonful of brown sugar; a piece of kohlrabi; a bit of ersatz honey; a bit of ersatz paprika powder; a small glass with barklike noodles in it; a tiny flask of vegetable oil; a dish of coffee-grime. On a piece of paper lay a pair of saccharine tablets and several *Irisen*, a plate of radish leaves and another of cabbage leaves.

The flies danced about in a circle.

Near the window, the merchant lay on a bed in death throes. He was only skin and bones; what was left was devoured by lice. The bedclothes were ringed about with flies and stains from smeared bedbugs. . . .

Inside the house stood a small boy—naked as the day his mother bore him. The child was not as poor, God forbid, as when he left his mother's womb. Heaven forfend! For how is it possible that the Almighty should abandon a little child? A Jewish child in particular! The child possessed a wealth of scrofula sores which, knock on wood, blossomed all over him, from head to toe. Standing in the streak of sunlight which was lighting up the flying dust as in a cotton mill, the child was warming himself.

Shloime Zabludovitch turned aside with a spasm of pain in his chest, too upset to look—and went on on his swollen feet. He was coming closer to the street of the dye works. He could tell which color was being painted today by the appearance of the gutters. A young man ran past him on the sidewalk, crying: "I'm starving! I'm starving! Have pity, give me something to eat! I'm starving!"

He snatched up a pebble from the ground and tried, without success, to chew it, hurled away the pebble, and continued running and crying out: "I'm starving! I'm starving! Jews! For the sake of heaven!"

Another demonstration, Zabludovitch thought, of his great good luck in having a cat—and that he would soon have bread.

We leave Zabludovitch now on his way to pick up the cat at the factory, and make our way into the factory to see what has been going on there.

In the "antechamber" of the factory stand large kettles of soup, brought over from the kitchen, and two women "vigilantes" (dispensers) are waiting impatiently.

To become a dispenser—a server—in a kitchen you had to have plenty of pull. A dispenser didn't go hungry. Some of the "consumers" bribed them with gold, diamonds, expensive linens, clothes, shoes, just to get a bigger portion of soup. The dispenser looked each consumer in the eye before she ladled out the bit of soup. They appeared very healthy and were very insolent.

The antechamber is an old wooden shack that leaks when it rains. The walls are tacked up with paper, not to keep the cold from blustering in, but to keep the light from pouring out during the night, because of the blackout—to keep from being punished by banishment from the ghetto to a certain death, as often happened, for allowing the smallest streak of light to escape into the dark.

Near the window that faces out to the yard of the factory stands a table and a broken chair. Here sits the porter. Against the wall stands a broken-down old bench supported by rocks; on one side, a barrel of water with two pails painted red. One pail is for water—and the other has a pump and a hose. Nearby, a box of sand. A white sign hangs on the wall over it, with the letters, L.S.W. for *Luftschutz Wache* (Air-Defense Watch). A bit higher hangs the portrait of the "Kaiser" of the ghetto, Rumkowski.

In the center is an oven with a crooked pipe secured with wires to the rafter to keep it from falling off. Winters, when the fire in the oven is kindled for heat, it is hard to draw a breath; when the oven fails, it is colder indoors than out.

The round clock hanging on the wall governs the lives of the workers: a few minutes late, and you're not admitted into the factory, you don't get any soup, and you're considered a deserter. For that, the punishment is deportation and certain death.

They eat their soup by the clock and they go home by the clock.

The workers of the factory are now focusing all their thoughts on the clock of the "antechamber" to induce it to call them to get their bit of soup at last.

The two dispensers in white aprons with little white kerchiefs on their heads are standing there, their eyes in their round well-fed faces looking nervously at the clock as they count the minutes. They still have to go to many other factories to dispense soup.

Finally, both hands of the clock meet on twelve and the ancient clock commences groaning.

The porter grabs hold of the rusty iron pipe, opens the little window, and unsteadily strikes the steel railing suspended with a wire on the outside wall with all his might. "Cling-clang! Cling-clang!" The workers spill through the doors of the factory, cups in hand.

Everyone wants to get at his bit of soup first, having dreamed about it for the past twenty-four hours. They run with all their strength, jumping over one another. Rushing, shoving, creating a hullabaloo, a deafening din, and in the blink of an eye a long line appears. Jars, pots, cups fly in all directions, over heads and hands, eyes wildly flashing, teeth grinding murderously. Cries echo resoundingly:

"Let me through!"

"I got here ahead of you!"

"But I've had no bread today!"

"What about me? I haven't had a thing to eat all day!"

"Get out of here or I'll split your head open with your own pot!"

"Pfui, pfui," he spits in his face and totters back to the end of the line like a drunk.

At the little window:

A young boy, skin and bones, in torn and dirty clothing, wearing heavy wooden shoes, speaks with the voice of a young hen: "Yesterday you gave me two soups and all I could find in them were two tiny shreds of potato, no larger than a tiny nut. And when I bit into them I thought I was gassed they stank so bad!"

An old Jew wearing a long kaftan so soiled it might just have been pulled up out of the mud, moans weakly, and speaks in a voice that weakness has rendered hoarse: "I beg you, please, give me a good portion! It's all I have to live on. God will bless you for your charity."

"Come on now, enough! Shove off! It's my turn to get some of that stuff," the blond Yablonka shouts out in rhyme. "Wow, is she a knockout, this server. And look at how she serves! As I live, and as she lives too!"

No doubt he hopes that his compliment would get him a special bowl of soup. But where would she get a thick soup for everyone? The total amount is allocated so that there would be a few pieces of kohlrabi and sometimes a few bits of potato per head. Yablonka the redhead shoves his bent head through the little window and his eyes rest on the soup kettle: "My dear woman, I'm not joking—ladle it out a little deeper and a little thicker." With the speed of lightning he snatches back the bowl and puts it to his mouth. His tongue makes a quick trip from the bottom of the bowl and up, so as not to lose a single tear of soup the dispenser might have shed in ladling it. Then he licks all around the edge of the bowl and takes a few gulps. He does all this in the blink of an eye. Then, taking the spoon he has been holding ready in one hand all this time, he shoves it into the bowl and starts counting the potatoes. And as though he has just been scalded, he yells out: "Woe is me! My grief is great! Pure water! Kohlrabi piss! They gobble up the potatoes themselves! I hope they bust their guts!"

Nine-year-old Moishele fell upon a clever plan: into his own bowl he set a false bottom with tiny holes like a sieve, and in the middle he set a small stick. Walking over to the window he is silent, uttering not a single word. As soon as the woman dispensing the soup returns his bowl of soup, he pulls out the false bottom and shoves it in front of her unbelieving eyes. The false bottom speaks for him: "See how you've cheated me"—and she has no choice but to add a few more pieces of kohlrabi or potatoes.

Little Bernstein, whose whole family was taken from him by the Germans during the "Curfew," and who managed to hide in a barrel full of feathers in the attic, has his own philosophy: the soup at the bottom of the kettle must be denser. So he endures the wait and always goes last. When he gets his bowl back and stirs the soup with his spoon, he is terribly let down. He cannot find a single piece of potato—it had all been ladled out before he got there. He pleads with the dispenser to give him a little extra soup instead. She wavers, since she is only given a determined number of allotted portions herself, but the seven-year-old little orphan arouses her compassion, and on her own responsibility she ladles out an additional half-portion into his bowl. As pleased with himself as though he had just conquered the world, the little tyke takes off.

Everyone runs and eats at the same time. Each one searches out his own little corner, and holding their bowls between their feet they wipe them clean with their fingers and lick them with their tongues as if the bowls contained some great delicacy. Then, licking the spoons clean and tucking the bowls under their arms, they all gravitate to the guardhouse—like cats—to grab a kettle and scrape out the sides and bottoms for any leftovers.

As soon as the dispensers leave with the pots, all the workers gather together in a corner of the plant and commence the daily discussion: about rations, about the extras that were dealt out—not for hard workers, not for the sick, but for those with pull.

Yablonka, the redhead, jokes around: "Want to hear a story about pull? I was hanging around in the cooperative, and I saw a butcher pinch a girl's backside. Well, well, you should have heard her turn on him and yell: "What do you think you're doing pinching my shoulders?" and he answered: "That's not your shoulders!" "Excuse me," she said, "that's where my pull comes from!"

Everyone burst out laughing, including Yablonka, who cuts across the general hilarity with the words: "You can laugh! Pull here, pull there, it's become impossible to contain your hunger!"

"*Oy*," sighs a woman. "If the Germans would just send us some potato peel we could make pancakes, baked beans, *cholent!*"

Esther Estreich, twenty-two, was sent into the ghetto of Lodz from Zonska Wola, and cries endlessly for her whole family butchered at the cemetery by the Germans before her eyes. Today she has brought several recipes for a variety of salads, tarts, and beefsteak from kohlrabi peelings.

Everyone dreams of kohlrabi peelings. Only the blond Yablonka, who has a face like an ailing tomato and whose skin is scaling, breaks into the dream with, "Saccharin must be added to all these recipes—then it'll taste like ambrosia! Everyone knows that!" Of course, Yablonka himself is the only dealer in saccharin. Wherever he is, he sings out in a melody of his own devising: "Saccharin! Four for one mark. Saccharin!" And he claims that his wife cooks rice for him made of radish which is so tasty—he doesn't need anything better!

They all become very curious—"How does she do it?" several inquire, hands outstretched. And he answers: "I can give you the recipe." The *yekke* Jews take out their notebooks and pens; the Polish Jews rely on their memories. Yablonka continues, "Take a radish and peel it, because the skin is tough, then grate it against the heavy grater and salt it. Set a pot of water to boil, and when the water's boiling—toss the radish in, let it cook for fifteen minutes, serve it on a platter, and you have rice—real, true rice! May I live to survive the war! And the broth tastes like a fine chicken broth! To say nothing if you have to boot some pre-war sugar beans! I tell you, I wouldn't want my enemies to know the taste of such a delicacy!"

Pinyele *Mazik* (Mischiefmaker): so called because of his wild pranks; he is also called "Gimpy" because he drags along on crutches. He should have been taking Vigantol to strengthen his bones and be able to walk. He is all of sixteen, and looks ancient. When people say: "Gimpy, you poor thing, you need Vigantol for your feet," he answers, "Who, me? Let's send some to the Red Army, so they can get here faster, then my feet'll get well in a hurry!" Pinyele has a dark head of hair, black eyes, a longish nose, and a beautifully chiseled face. He is bent with a hunched back; in addition, he has recently developed a few holes in his lungs. The doctors informed him that he must eat well, have plenty of fresh air, and drink lots of cod-liver oil. But he can only dream about all that. He often sings a little *gemora* to himself: "*Hakol shochtin*—everyone may slaughter! Is that the reason the Germans slaughter us?" Out of habit, he sings in his resonant voice, stretching the syllables. He keeps complaining: "The war made a heretic of me. I quarreled with heaven. Life in the ghetto taught me that there is no God! Would a father torture his children so even for the worst sins imaginable? We're supposed to be God's children! He has made an ocean of human blood of his lovely world, and he ordered his children to gobble each other up!"

"Pinyele *Mazik*! Bite your tongue!" old Tsirl scolds him. "For saying things like that you can be damned forever!"

"No! Speak on, Gimpy, you're right!" the red-blond Yablonka encourages him, adding fuel to the fire.

This very Pinyele *Mazik* has brought a new recipe today. "Listen to me attentively!" he sings out with a *gemora* melody. "From the coffee-grime can be concocted the finest recipes! *Tsimmes*, tarts, pancakes, baked beans!"

"What's that? Of coffee-grime?"—Red Yablonka mocks him.

But Pinyele *Mazik* continues: "Why do I have to eat the coffee right out of the sack?"—turning his forefinger in the air as if he had asked a *gemora* question, he answers himself: "I take half a pot of coffee-grime, pour in a little water, a teaspoon of oil, a few saccharin tablets, flour if I have any, then I pour some sugar over it, and it's a *tsimmes*. You can also grate some potato into it, if you have any, a teaspoon of flour, if you have any, and you can bake the very best cookies. In winter, if you happen to have a frozen potato or a frozen kohlrabi, you can make delicious tarts of the coffee-grime. I tell you, I wouldn't want my enemies to taste anything like that."

Red Yablonka remarks that the coffee-grime hurts his tongue, his throat, his lungs, his heart, his whole body and his whole life.

So Pinyele *Mazik* retorts that being that he is such a delicate and refined person he, Pinyele, has some advice for him: sieve it through a strainer.

And Yablonka responds: "For me, Gimpy, you don't have to go to the trouble of discovering America—all that's left after you strain a whole kilo of coffee-grime is ten decas, all dregs, only fit to throw into the garbage. But, if you don't strain it, it just slithers down like a roast."

And now comes Hubert. His face is glowing. He is a Jew from Prague. Hitler reminded him that he is a Jew and he was deported to the ghetto of Lodz. Hubert is still elegantly clad. Before the war he was the editor of a daily newspaper and later the owner of several movie houses. Here in the ghetto, he goes about with one idea: promptly upon liberation, he would start the cameras rolling for a film about the ghetto of Lodz. He has already commissioned a scenario from a certain man of letters who works in the factory. A romance must also be woven into the story of the ghetto involving a beautiful young girl. And something about him and his wife as well—his wife, who, although she was not Jewish, came to the ghetto with him and suffers just as much. Hubert is a strong believer that Hitler's death is just around the corner.

When everyone ran to get their soup, Hubert ran to get the latest news from Radio London.

First thing in the morning before starting for work, every Jew donates one mark so that at the first stroke of the midday bell Hubert can race to get the news from the underground radio. Jews know that this is tied up with a great deal of money and even danger to life and limb, but for the latest news, the ghetto Jew is prepared to lose his dearest possession.

As soon as Hubert arrives, everyone crowds around him. His first words: "Good news!" And he relays a report from the eastern front and from the western front, skipping no detail, including the announcer's comments. Everyone admires his keen mind. Then he gives his own commentary. Listening to him is like reading a newspaper. A discussion soon follows among the members of the audience—optimists versus pessimists. Hubert speaks quite calmly. "The Germans are retreating in great confusion from the eastern front. They are surrounded on every side, and the ground is mined under their feet wherever they move."

Fresh hope is awakened and warms the Jews' hearts.

"All of Germany is being bombed night and day! Entire cities are razed! Not a stone in Hamburg's ruins is left standing on another! The western front will soon be opened!"

Here's where the discussion gets warm. They vie to outdo one another with optimistic comments:

"If only one lives, one lives to see everything!"

"Well, what did I tell you?"

"Only faith is needed," puts in old Reb Chaim Silverberg, a former manufacturer, a scholar, who is esteemed even here. He lingers over every word, *gemora*-fashion. "The war may be over at any moment. Italy has already surrendered, right? And the axis is broken, right? Can a wagon roll with a broken axle?"

"It will soon be over and with the help of the Almighty we'll be going home!" old Lande shouts enthusiastically.

Yablonka the redhead can't abide the sight of this fatuous calflike enthusiasm, and cries out: "Talk is cheap! I have no faith in the thieving British! They'd just love to see both sides drown in blood and then march in over their graves. And of course over ours too! It's not as easy as you think!"

"W-W-What's that?" they all fall on him at once. "Sure! You want the war to go on for years! You have time to wait? Wait. We don't! Are you so happy here?"

"The whole trouble really is," Yablonka replies, "that we Jews can't wait. Oh, no. The slaughtering knife is pointed right over here"—and he points to his own throat. "You really believe in a western front very soon? England is a cold-blooded murderer: England will fight to the last Russian soldier!"

"*Oy*, Yablonka, even a hunchback's hump doesn't grow up to the sky!" yells Pinyele.

"And a crutch doesn't grow into the earth!" Lande screams back still louder, and Pinyele feels embarrassed as everyone laughs.

"England will chop them to bits like a herring!" prophesies old Silverberg, "and wipe the Nazis off the map! And this is absolutely the last war."

"True, true," Yablonka responds, "that must be so because in his last speech Churchill really threatened the Germans."

Now they're all very curious and they surround him, listening. Yablonka finishes in a single breath:

"He warned them that unless they surrendered he would show them! He would be forced immediately to make another speech!". . . .

The redhead's final words hit them like a cold shower. They stood perplexed, as Yablonka continued:

"You know when the western front will be opened? When the Red Army will be standing by Berlin. I'll tell you something else. You really believe they'll avenge themselves on the Nazis? Never! Because this is not the last war, Reb Silverberg. No, sir! Every last one of them will make up to the Nazis, because they'll need them for future wars, ha, ha; it's going to take plenty of time to wipe out the murderers."

Tsirl was an old woman who was the only one of her entire family to survive and could not understand how she had managed to evade so many "selections." Now Tsirl sighs, "All our shrouds are going to waste. We are rocking a dead child!"

"You people, you're suffering because you're Jews," calls out Kraus, the baptized Jew's grandson. "Why am I suffering? I'm pure German—a *Reichsdeutscher*—and the stupid Nazis stuck me away here in the ghetto. *Donnerwetter! Ich bin kein Jude! Ich bin Reichsdeutsche!*" he screams hysterically.

"Sure, sure, Herr Kraus—" Silberberg says to him. "Sure, it makes no difference these days even if it was only your grandfather who was a Jew—albeit an apostate. Poor man, you've lost both worlds: you won't, you can't, live with us, and they won't let you live with them.... At least we know why we're suffering. They're killing us because we're Jews."

Pinyele *Mazik*'s voice rings out with a talmudic *nigun*:

"*Oy*, Jews, what's the use of all this philosophizing, if hunger torments us. The important thing is a piece of bread! Let the war be a war, we need bread! *Oy*, if the war ends, my first act will be to turn to the nearest bakery and grab a loaf and eat and eat until once and for all I'm no longer hungry!"

"Me too! Me too!" everyone yells in one voice.

"Oh you Gimpy!" breaks in Yablonka, "you poor thing, you haven't got an ounce of sense: Today's war is a war against Jews! Do our brothers in America at least know of our plight?" and he sighs audibly. "I have a rich uncle in Brooklyn, and besides, how am I to know that Jews are secure in America? I fear that our brethren in America are also living in fear; I am convinced they're doing everything possible to help us, but the wicked world prevents them!"

"That," answers Pinyele *Mazik*, "can only happen to a people that has no land of its own. If we Jews don't get our own country after the war, may the whole world go to the devil!"

"Gimpy, tremors you can get, a hole in your lungs, a hernia!" Yablonka yells at him. "But a country? A country has to be won by its people!"

Old Silberberg consoles him: "This war," he says piously, "is a war against the Jewish spirit! Against the ten commandments! Against the spirit of our ancient prophets!" He takes a deep breath. Everything is still. "Gold, gold," he continues, "gold! the

Jewish people is likened to gold; the more you refine it, the better it gets, the more precious, the purer!" Turning to Pinyele, "Even though they've been trying to destroy us for two thousand years, we have still remained a nation. Above all, young man, faith! This already is the war of Gog and Magog! You can see it, it's evident that redemption is close by! Faith, Jews! Faith! The Red Army is cutting down the Nazis like grass!"

Tsirl groans: "Whoever has a bit of bread will survive to welcome the Messiah."

"Zabludovitch will live to see the Messiah," old Lande shouts, "He has a cat; oh, he'll have bread today all right!" he adds enviously.

"True, true," confirms old Silverberg. "A cousin of mine told me that in his plant he heard his foreman tell about a man who caught a cat, and took the cat into the administration building, and was given a whole loaf of bread for her, on the spot."

Everybody now envies the "man" and each ponders: "Where and how had he gotten a loaf of bread in exchange for the cat?"

The red-blond Yablonka remarks that he would be able to cure his eczema in one day just from the pieces of fat his cat sneaked out of the kitchen. "But where are you now, my dearest kitty?" and his words are heartfelt. "You would have been able to repay me with a whole loaf of bread!"

He stands still for a while, musing, absorbed in his thoughts, then bursts into hearty laughter and everyone joins in.

When Zabludovitch arrived at the street where the factory stood, various thoughts raced through his mind: "What if the cat wasn't there? Maybe that *yekke* made himself a cat roast during the night! Maybe the laundress stole the cat!" he sighed apprehensively, and burdened with these thoughts, he made for the factory. On the threshold, the supervisor confronted him with a loud outcry: "Mister Zabludovitch, if you don't take your cat away this instant, I'll let her loose myself, right now. How can a Jew torture one of God's creatures like that? To keep her in a sack all night! A man who feels for all living things! The cat will perish! I think she's dead already! Yes, I clean forgot, she's dead already! Instead of bread you have a dead cat!"

Zabludovitch's heart stopped beating.

Bewildered, he ran into the factory. Everyone was looking at him and Lande said secretively: "D'you hear? The cat is here, he hid her someplace." And old Silverberg added, "Does he really think we're going to let him take her out of here?"

The dye works consisted of one large workshop. Several huge iron and wooden vats as well as a bath stood in this room. It was into these vats that the workers threw the bloodied underwear of the massacred Jews, and stirred them with sticks until they were cooked through and dyed. Then the merchandise was shipped off to the carpet department. Jews were put to work weaving the dyed underwear into rugs for the Germans. The floor of the factory was completely covered with blood-soaked underthings. . . . The entire factory was permeated with a penetrating stench.

When Zabludovitch walked into the dye works, he beheld the ticking lying on the same mound of bloodied rags where he set it down the day before, and he could hear meowing. . . . He felt a load drop from his shoulders. Immediately he snatched up the cat and on his swollen feet danced a little jig on the bloody rags. But now old Silverberg grabbed hold of his shoulder and addressed him in *gemora*-study singsong:

"Mister Zabludovitch, please be kind enough not to rush! We who work in this chamber have decided that the cat belongs to all of us. You cannot take a larger share than we. The cat was caught in this room—right? We all saw it. It is written in the Talmud: Whoever finds a precious article must share it with whoever saw him pick it up. The cat wandered into this room yesterday, and we saw the woman catch her. So you will pardon me, and be kind enough to wait. All of us will go to the food administration together. These days, bread can't be entrusted to any one person. This is a ghetto!"

A few workers joined him. They began to bicker among themselves. Zabludovitch wailed loudly: "No! I'm not giving up the cat! She's mine!" The women shrieked. Suddenly the engineer came into the room. Everyone sidled over to his job and Zabludovitch sidled out with the cat.

Zabludovitch was making his way to the food administration. The cat writhed about and meowed. Zabludovitch was covered from head to toe with feathers from the mattress ticking. Fearful that someone might, God forbid, tear the cat away from him, he squeezed her still closer beneath his arm. People were stopping and staring after him with curiousity and envy, and pointing:

"*Oy*, a cat! He'll be getting bread!"

Children trailed after him, crying:

"A cat, a cat! Bwead, bwead!"

Zabludovitch was too embarrassed to look up.

Near the administration building an envious crowd had gathered. The street turned black with people. Zabludovitch had deliberated on the possible danger of returning to this street with bread.

He stumbled blindly into the anteroom of the administration building.

"Where are you running to like a madman?" he heard someone call out. It took him a good second or two before he was aware of anyone.

"I need the manager, Herr Shtchenshlivi, or the supervisor," Zabludovitch answered, confused.

"The supervisor?—I'm the supervisor! What is it?"

"I brought a cat."

"Well, what do you want for her?"

"What do you think I want for her? A loaf of bread!"

"Ha-ha-ha! A loaf of bread? Give me a loaf of bread and I'll give you twenty cats! Four-legged and two-legged! Ten marks is all I can give for her. Do you want it?"

Zabludovitch felt himself sinking to the ground. He prayed for the earth to open up and swallow him.

Could he leave now with the cat? The people who waited for him outside would tear him to bits. Should he take the ten marks? His partner wouldn't believe it and would accuse him of stealing the bread. At this point it occurred to him that the "Tier-Zucht" foreman had promised him a large, beautiful, fresh egg. "How many years is it," he thought, "since I last saw a fresh egg? I'm sure to get a piece of bread in exchange for the egg, and the watchman, David Klepsidre, promised to give me a half kilo of bread. I'll sell the cat to either one of them; let them come down here—they're the ones with pull!" And turning to the supervisor, he said:

"My dear Mr. Supervisor, sir, I have a great favor to ask of you. Would you show me the courtesy of showing me through a different exit going out to the other street? Because out there"— and he motioned to the door through which he had just come in—"the street is black with the crowds of people just waiting for me and the cat."

The supervisor accomodated him.

When Shloime Zabludovitch arrived back at his own house he undid the ticking and released the cat. He looked her over reflectively: her beautiful coat of snow-white fur with black and brown spots, beautiful white whiskers, light green eyes with black pupils like stripes down the center. She contracted so that her back arched up like a hillock, and repeated it several times. Feeling sorry for her, he unlocked his valise and took out a large bag tightly wrapped and corded around about ten times. He cut a morsel of bread from his own wretched portion and, weighing it in his hand as he sliced, he said to himself: "On account of this cat we robbed ourselves of our own portions yesterday."

The cat sniffed all over the bit of bread and didn't eat it.

"Oh, what have I done! I made the cat sick!" he worried, "Keeping her in that sack all night...."

He brushed the feathers off his clothes and ran to get the sausage ration. He made a quick stop at the "Tier-Zucht" and informed the watchman that he now had the cat. The watchman told him to bring her right in and he would run down to the administration building to get the bread, and they would share it. Because, these days, who would hand out bread in advance? Zabludovitch then went to the foreman for an egg, only to have to listen to the same reply.

Zabludovitch returned home with twenty decas (200 grams) of horsemeat sausage. This was a month's supply—ten decas a head. He cut off a piece of bread and a tiny piece of sausage to allay his hunger. He threw the cat a piece of the skin. She sniffed around and didn't eat. "My God! I've really gotten her sick!" he thought.

The sunlight streamed in through the window. The cat leaped up onto the sill—and sat washing and warming herself. Unable to control himself, Zabludovitch cut himself another morsel of bread and another piece of the sausage, swallowing it down like a pill. He glanced at the clock: it was half past one already and he had to rush to work, so he hurriedly put the bread back into the valise, wrapped and tied the sausage securely in its linen bag, cheerful at the thought that his wife would prepare a fine goulash for dinner that evening. Leaving it all sitting on the table, he grabbed the bucket and went out to get some water. His hand resting on the doorknob, he took another look at the cat. "What a tidy creature she is! How nicely she washes herself!"

On the way back with the water, he noticed that the cat was no longer seated on the window sill. As he came in the door, there she was back in the same position as when he left.

He put the bucket back, and cast a glance at the table—disaster! The bag was torn to shreds and half the sausage was missing.

He was overcome with anguish. Running over to the cat he yelled at her, his eyes filled with tears: "So that's it, you're really a thief, are you!? There's no doubt you come from a wealthy home! You're used to gobbling up meat. All this time I thought I made you sick!"

Hitting the cat with one hand he pointed at the sausage with the other: "What have you done?"

The cat lowered her head, as though she knew and felt guilty.

He took the knife and trimmed the sausage and put it into the valise, consoling himself meanwhile: "At least my wife's portion is still here. I'll just pretend Rumkowski didn't give out any sausage rations this time." He regretted having eaten up today's portion of bread yesterday, and that he had to go to work without eating. "Some cat, a calamity!" he called out, slamming shut the door and dragging himself off to work on his swollen feet.

When Zabludovitch came into the factory all the workers, with his partner at their head, were waiting for him with great curiousity: What had he brought in exchange for the cat?

Zabludovitch recited the whole truth.

"They would only give me ten marks for the cat, so I took her home with me."

He spoke for his partner's benefit, so that she wouldn't claim half a bread. He wasn't worried about the workers because they hadn't expected him to share with them from the outset.

"You can't trust anyone these days," his partner said. "This is a ghetto. Give me the cat. Even though I'm so weak I can barely set one foot before the other, I'll manage to sell her myself. Men just aren't good for things like that. Wait and see, I'll get the bread and we'll share it," she groaned.

They decided that he would bring the cat the following day and deliver it into her hands.

At this point old Lande came walking in, besmirched as a chimney sweep, and puffing away on a pipeful of cherry leaves.

As usual, he had a coughing spasm, and let loose with an ample, "A-a-ah! Good-morning, Mr. Zabludovitch! Well, how did you make out with the cat? Bread taste good? Honest weight? Only bread, or money too?"

Each word was salt to Zabludovitch's open wounds. He was still suffering from the loss of the sausage the cat had eaten and the bread he had eaten himself the day before. Now he was dying of hunger and ashamed to admit it. So he answered angrily:

"My dear Mr. Lande, let me be! All they were going to give me for the cat was ten marks! So don't bother me! Why don't you go and attend to your own things?"

"W-w-ha-at? T-t-e-n marks? Whom are you trying to fool? Ten marks will get you two saccharin tablets today! A loaf of bread costs 1,800 marks! Whom do you think you're fooling? That's the way it goes today: one has a bread and he becomes a high-and-mighty muckamuck! Afraid I begrudge you the bread? Eat it with a good appetite! If you weren't so lucky, would I be less hungry? I ask just one thing: Don't take me for a lunatic! My name, you know, is Lande!"

"I'm telling you, Mr. Lande," Zabludovitch persisted, "that the food administration doesn't need any cats. They have plenty of cats—four-legged and two-legged! That's what the supervisor told me!"

"Of course, they've got enough of two-legged cats! There's Shtchenshlivi and Rheingold—*Rheinschmaltz* they call him— round and roly-poly as a barrel! And the rest of those crooks? They're eating us all up alive! Just wait till our moment comes and the wires are ripped out—that's when we'll settle our accounts with those two-legged cats, those bloodsuckers! But they are short of four-legged cats! That's what they're buying! And don't think to make me look like a fool! I'm a bit older than you and I hate lies!"

In the evening his wife brought Zabludovitch a little soup. She knew he was too hungry to wait until he was through with work:

after all, he hadn't even had his bread that day, she realized when she looked into the bag that he had locked away in the valise. (She always cut the bread she got at the cooperative into eight portions—for eight days.) She began telling Zabludovitch what a clever creature the cat was: she had barely opened the door when the cat ran up to her, meowing, winding herself around Hannele's feet, until she led her to the valise. The cat scratched at the valise, looking into her eyes as though to say: "I'm hungry, there's food in there, please give me some." Hannele opened the valise and gave her a bit of bread. The cat sniffed it up and down and wouldn't eat it. She gave her a piece of skin from the sausage, and the cat sniffed at that too. She cried, watching Hannele eat, and Mrs. Zabludovitch was so touched with compassion for the cat that she gave her a tiny piece of sausage. "Isn't that the cleverest cat?"

Zabludovitch answered that the cat seemed to have come from a wealthy home or from a butcher. And to himself he thought: at least she asked Hannele, but me she simply robbed. Gulped down my whole sausage. Some cat, she's a disaster! "Listen Hannele," he blurted out, "the food administration doesn't need any cats. They wanted to give me ten marks for her, no more!"

When Zabludovitch and his wife returned home, they found the door broken open. First things first, they ran to check the valise to make sure their bit of food was still there. Everything was in order, but—the cat had been stolen.

They couldn't go to sleep until the lock had been repaired. How could anyone leave a house unlocked in the ghetto? Nearly everyone worked all day—and even at night? Was there a shortage of volunteers, then, lurking about for food?

Zabludovitch went for a locksmith. The locksmith wouldn't even go near the job until he was paid ten decas of bread—"I don't accept money! Money has no value these days! All I want for my labor is ten decas of bread!" he argued as he removed a wrench from his toolbox.

Zabludovitch explained about his bad luck: The door was only broken open on account of the cat. It was just a miracle that his food hadn't been stolen as well.

The locksmith only had to hear the word "cat," and was infuriated: "Serves you right! To leave a cat alone in the house these days! A cat is equivalent to a loaf of bread! Give me a cat and I'll make you fifty locks! A cat should be guarded as carefully as the eyes in your head!"

With great lamentation, Zabludovitch cut and weighed ten decas of bread. Every cut of the knife pierced him to the heart.

In the morning, when Zabludovitch arrived at the factory, his partner was waiting for the cat.

He told her of the theft. She refused to believe him: Everyone was saying that he got a whole loaf of bread which he didn't want to share with her, so he thought up this story.

Old Silverberg mourned: "Never in all my life would I have believed that Zabludovitch could be such a fraud. Such a schemer." His ex-partner ran at him with fists raised, crying hysterically: "How could you take the bread right out of the mouths of my poor unfortunate orphans! You murderer!"

And old Lande was busily pointing out to everyone how clever a Jew he was: "Well?" he asked, "You may be handsome, but I have brains. These days you can't trust anyone with bread. This is a ghetto!"

It was decided that Zabludovitch was a cheat and a swindler. Fruitlessly Zabludovitch swore: "May I live to see the day of Hitler's downfall!" The cat stole from him, and then the cat herself was stolen, and now he was being taken for a miserable liar!

He turned away and standing in a corner, silently, so that no one would see him, silently he wept. . . .

Suddenly the door to the street swung open and Klepsidre shuffled in on all fours, his hands against the wall, a sack under one arm: "Mister Zabludovitch, where are you?!—" he croaked— "Here, here's your cat."

Zabludovitch, who was still standing facing the wall wiping away his tears, cried out tearfully, "Oh, dear Lord, why are they tormenting me?"

The red-blond Yablonka pushed a chair over for Klepsidre who sank into it. Breathing heavily he glanced down at his feet, and seeing how swollen they were, he sighed mournfully. As he handed over the sack to Zabludovitch, the cat commenced to cry: "Meow, meow, meow." Zabludovitch turned quickly toward him with astonishment written all over his face, and didn't take the cat. Klepsidre defended himself, squeezing out every word, and breathing hard like a dying man:

"I thought that . . . I'd be able to get some bread for my sick wife and sick children and I wanted to be a partner with the cat. I've just come from the food administration, they wouldn't give me anything!"

He paused, looking everyone in the eyes sharply to ascertain the effect of his words. When he saw that they were all listening attentively, he continued in the tone of a man who proposes some great plan to save his country from catastrophe:

"Know then! The administration has no need of cats!!! May the tongue of the perpetrator of this lie dry up in his mouth and fall off!" He cursed in his fury and had a coughing spell.

Shloime Zabludovitch, who promised himself to tear the thief in pieces, was ready to embrace Klepsidre, but was embarrassed before the assemblage. He took the cat from him and gave it over to Mrs. Hershkowitz who couldn't look him in the face and was motionless. Zabludovitch lay the bag down on the bench and said: "Well, kitty, now you're not even worth as much as a parsnip root!"

No one made a move toward the cat. They couldn't face one another, and one by one they shuffled off into the factory.

The cat lowered herself to the floor, and creeping the length and breadth of the sack, she cried: "Meow, meow, meow!" searching for a way to freedom.

Zabludovitch's heart ached with pity for the cat. He really wanted to free her, but, "I'm not her owner," he told himself. He glanced at the woman, his ex-partner, and she was sitting and grieving, causing him to feel even greater compassion.

Suddenly Mrs. Hershkowitz got up, and quickly untied the sack. Zabludovitch couldn't take his eyes off her. She took out the cat, and opened wide the door to the street: "Have a long life and go in peace!" Saying this she let the cat go free. The cat leaped out of her hands and ran and ran.

Zabludovitch's face lit up with a happy smile.

Soon the street resounded with the clamor of people chasing after the cat.

A CUPBOARD
in the
GHETTO

Hershel Zeif was an emaciated man with a pale, peaked face and lustreless eyes. A native of Kalisz, he had been married in Lodz just before the war. He and his wife, luckily, were able to bring with them into the Ghetto their entire wedding outfit, all their clothes, as well as twin beds, a table, several chairs and a clothes cupboard.

For a long time Hershel Zeif ran to the Civil Administration every day looking for work. After a while he became exasperated with the false promises of the officials and decided that if you had no "shoulders" (protection) you couldn't get anything. Now he and his wife spend most of the day in bed—he in one of the twin beds, she in the other—writhing from hunger and cold, like all their neighbors.

Pull?

Mrs. Zeif was small and thin, with hollow cheeks and big black eyes. She was a quiet woman who never raised her voice. Silently, within herself, she endured the grief and agony of hunger and cold. Both she and her husband were positive that the war would end any day.

When the sun rose higher and lavished its rays, also brightening their window, Hershel and his wife hung their wedding clothes out to air. There was Zeif's black winter coat with a velvet collar; a blue kapotte with a vent in back; trousers with a crease and cuffs; a pair of boots and a pair of shoes; a half-dozen white shirts; undershirts; a pair of soft leather bedroom slippers and a hard black hat, round as a coin, with a crescent brim like a new moon.

Mrs. Zeif had a black winter coat; a light summer coat; a suit; several dresses; a plush hat and a hand-knitted hat; underclothes, linens and four pairs of shoes.

All these things were brand new, they had never been worn. They were coated with green mildew. After several days in the sun the mildew whitened and then vanished. But after a few days in the house the green mildew appeared again. They decided to air their wedding clothes every day, sunny or not, just as long as it didn't rain. They made a pact: one day he hung his clothes outside the sunny window for several hours—the next day she hung hers. The sun never reached the other window, because it was in a corner opposite a high wall.

When Zeif saw that the mildew was gone, a smile of pleasure lit up his haggard face: "Yes, the war might end any minute. God can do anything, and we'll go home in our new clothes. Yes, yes, my dear Henye."

His wife nodded in agreement: "That's right!"

Hershel Zeif invited his neighbor Bluestein into his house. "Guess how my wife cooked supper today," he said in his weak voice, looking into Bluestein's eyes with a mischievous smile, like a schoolboy trying to confuse a friend with a difficult riddle.

Bluestein looked around, in all the corners, and saw that all was as before: the moldings of the door and windows and floor had long ago been swallowed up by the tiny kitchen stove. The floor itself could not be ripped up, because it was the second story and they could fall through. Besides, one of "Emperor"

Rumkowski's men came by every few days to inspect the floor. Bluestein also saw that the beds, the clothes cupboard, the table and chairs, were all there. The beds, by the way, were new and modern. The Zeifs had gotten them in exchange for their old oak beds, and were even paid for the difference in weight.

Bluestein wracked his brain. He wanted to guess the answer, he didn't want to be fooled.

"Come on, guess! You can't guess, can you?" Zeif teased him.

"I know!" Bluestein cried confidently. "With the board you got from the tinsmith!"

"Ha-ha! A likely story! Why don't you say with last year's snow? That board was used up long ago—even the ashes are gone," Zeif shouted triumphantly.

This was what had happened: it had rained in, and Zeif had to put pans on the beds. After much pleading, the administrator of the buildings in the neighborhood sent him a tinsmith to fix the roof. The tinsmith climbed into the attic, and immediately Zeif heard boards being pried loose over his head. Soon the tinsmith climbed down calmly, with a pile of boards under his arm. Zeif started to shout: "You're a robber! You've ruined me! I almost died until you finally got here! Instead of fixing the roof so it shouldn't rain in on me, you destroyed it and are taking home the wood!? You've made it worse! Don't you have any feelings?"

"Oh, come on now," the tinsmith replied calmly. "Why should you eat your heart out over such a little thing? The house isn't even yours. Until it rains again, the war might end. Look how hot it is. You know it rains very seldom in the summer, and when it does, it's hardly more than a drizzle. The roof doesn't even get wet. Anyway, we are having a dry summer, and by the fall we'll all have forgotten that there was ever a war, with a Ghetto, with an Emperor Rumkowski."

"God forbid that the war should last until the fall," Zeif interrupted him. "It's lasted almost two years already."

"Of course. Now take a board for yourself for fuel and it'll bring you luck—you'll see the end of the war," and he thrust a board under Zeif's arm.

Zeif thought: "As I live and breathe, the man is right." Aloud, he said: "What can I do with you? Shall I report you to the 'Emperor's' police? How can I?" He seized the board with both hands and pointed to Bluestein: "But *he's* the one you have to watch out for. He sees that nobody steals any wood."

The tinsmith grew a little frightened, but Bluestein looked at him pityingly and he felt better. Zeif added: "Don't be afraid. I should live so long what a nice man he is, huh, Mr. Bluestein? I swear he would never hurt anyone."

The tinsmith left quickly with his bundle and Zeif went into the house with the board and broke it into small pieces for several days' fuel.

"Mr. Bluestein, can you guess what my wife used for fuel when she cooked supper tonight? You can't guess, can you?"

"No," said Bluestein firmly.

Zeif opened the clothes cupboard with the expression of an inventor demonstrating his work. Bluestein saw that everything was ship-shape. The glassware, the china; even the paper shelving lay flat and smooth, and the linens were arranged in neat piles. Bluestein wondered: "What is he trying to show me?"

Zeif could no longer refrain from boasting. Quickly he lifted up the paper shelving and pointed: "See? Why do I need whole boards on the shelves? The wooden strips are enough." He cut an arc through the air with his thumb, chanting in Talmudist fashion: "So I removed the boards. I chopped up three boards, split two of them in strips, put four strips on each level, laid out the shelving paper with the clothes and all the rest of the things and there are my shelves. Can you tell the difference? Now my wife will be able to cook and cook for a long time." He pointed to the bunches of wood which he had divided into four tiny strips each. "More than that isn't necessary. I'm like 'Emperor' Rumkowski with his rations. I dole out rations to my wife. And thank God, we have what to cook." He showed Bluestein a big heap of cabbage roots.

Not far from Zeif's house there was a large field which the Agriculture Division had rented to one of Rumkowski's officials—formerly a rich man. After the cabbage was picked, Zeif dug out the roots, that were hard and bitter, and also took home the wild cabbage leaves that grew near the roots.

Two weeks later, Zeif called Bluestein again and said: "Well, be smart and guess with what my wife cooked her cabbage stew today!"

The same game was re-enacted. Bluestein pondered, searched, examined every corner of the house and couldn't find any clues to the riddle. Finally Zeif solved it for him. He flung open the door of the cupboard. "Why does a cupboard need a back wall when it stands against a wall? I removed the rest of the wall and now I'll have fuel for a long time."

From the roots and wild leaves Mrs. Zeif prepared appetizers, fish, meat, soups, tsimmes. She let the cabbage cook a while and then put in a lot of bicarbonate of soda, because soda boils up in hot water. She thought: it is cooking and at the same time the soda draws out the poisons. (The cabbage roots don't get soft even over the biggest fire.)

From the poison, Zeif made "marinated herring" (his own invention). He removed the bulbs from the roots, salted them heavily, and let them stand. Then he mixed a little vinegar and water, added some ersatz paprika and saccharin. Into this mixture, Zeif dipped his scrap of ersatz bread and sighed with pleasure: "Ah—ah—delicious," smacking his lips like in the good old days over a savory roast. He hummed a Chassidic tune, drumming his fingers on the table in rhythm. "Oh, a delicious marinated herring! Henye, our enemies should never enjoy it!" and his wife nodded in agreement as they ate with relish.

Two weeks later, Zeif called in Bluestein again and asked: "Well, guess how my wife cooked today? This time you must guess!" and he pointed to the cupboard that was covered with a blanket. "See? Today I got smarter! Why does a cupboard need a door? What's bad about this? Anything wrong? With the door my wife will be able to cook for a long time, and the cupboard is still a cupboard!"

Bluestein touched the cupboard with one finger and it began to sway back and forth.

Zeif defended the dignity of the cupboard: "That's nothing! Who's going to fight with it? A cupboard doesn't have to be strong, man!"

Bluestein's heart ached because of Zeif's decency—and agreed that he was a smart, practical man, a real inventor. Zeif tried to smile, but a grimace distorted his face.

The next day Mrs. Zeif, sobbing with terror, called in Bluestein: "Mr. Bluestein, look what's happened to my husband!"

Zeif lay in bed, unable to move. Overnight he had grown so swollen and his head and face so huge, that it covered the entire pillow. The bed was too narrow for his body.

Zeif said in a weak voice: "Look what happened to me! And all because I have no 'shoulders!'"

Bluestein tried to console him: "Don't worry, Mr. Zeif, the war will end any day now, and we'll go home together."

"Yes, Mr. Bluestein, my wife and I haven't even used up our wedding outfit."

"Listen to me, Mr. Zeif, sell some of your wedding clothes and buy yourself some bread and a bit of meat. When you get back to the city you'll get new clothes, maybe even better ones."

"We'll never sell anything from our wedding outfit. I just told you, we didn't even replace any of it. To spite the Germans we'll go home in those clothes!"

Bluestein didn't urge him, because he didn't want Zeif to doubt that the war would end any day. He said lightly:

"Don't worry about the swelling, it's nothing," but he was sure that Zeif would soon lose the battle with his hunger. At the door he said: "Mr. Zeif, in the middle of the night I'll come running in to tell you that the war is over!" and he left the house. He recalled that he had read in the forbidden *Deutsche Zeitung* the speech which Hans Greizer, may his name be blotted out, delivered to the Hitler youth on May 1, 1940, the day when the Ghetto was sealed off with barbed wire:

"The Jews are finished," Griezer said. "Hunger will turn them into mad dogs. They will bite chunks of flesh from each other. They will devour themselves!"

"It's true, we are dying out because of hunger," Bluestein thought, "but we have not become wild beasts. Not only are we not biting chunks of flesh from each other, but we don't even want to exchange a single garment from our wedding outfits for a piece of bread and meat. We don't steal and we don't kill. No, 'he' will not turn us into mad dogs! On the outside we look like corpses, but inside we have preserved the image of God."

Early next morning, Bluestein went to see how Hershel Zeif was feeling. He was afraid that Zeif had not lasted the night, or that he had taken his own life because of his suffering and despair.

But Bluestein was surprised! Overnight Zeif had grown as thin as a rail, and his skin was like that of a corpse. He couldn't get off the bed. Again Bluestein consoled him: "See, the swelling is gone! That's a good sign. You're getting better, you'll soon be well. Be patient, Mr. Zeif, we'll go home together."

"Oh, I haven't lost faith yet! What's this nonsense about my getting well soon? I'm not sick! I was never sick in my life! I'm just a little weak from hunger. I have pain—but that's nothing. The Hell with 'them'! Do you remember what Greizer, may his name be blotted out, said in those days? You should remember. He said: 'The Jews are finished.' Believe me, Mr. Bluestein, 'they' are finished! Last night I had a wonderful dream. I saw my father, of Blessed Memory, and—the war was over and I was beating up the Germans and 'Emperor' Rumkowski and his henchmen. How I took revenge! How I cooled my heart! I should be as sure of meeting my family again as I am sure that 'they' will die an unnatural death!" Zeif ranted in his weak voice.

"It's good, Mr. Zeif, good that you haven't lost faith! I admire you. You'll see, we'll go home together!"

Bluestein walked down the stairs with an aching heart, thinking: "Who knows what will happen to him? Hunger has already turned him into an obituary. The Angel of Death has placed his mark on him."

A little later Bluestein received the new ration, which contained two kilos of potatoes. He brought one kilo to the Zeifs: "Mrs. Zeif, I'm lending you a kilo of potatoes. When you get your ration you'll give it back. Cook the potatoes right away. They'll be good medicine for Zeif."

Husband and wife didn't know how to thank Bluestein. They showered blessings on him. With several slivers of wood, Mrs. Zeif boiled the potatoes half-raw in their skins. When they were eating, Henye tried to give the larger portion to Zeif and he tried to give the larger portion to her. After eating a few potatoes, Zeif felt better: "See, Henye, all we need is faith. With God's help we'll survive the war. Do you have any wood left for cooking?"

"Yes, for a few more times," she replied with satisfaction.

"See, Henye, the cupboard is still a cupboard," he smiled.

And they dipped the unpeeled potatoes in salt and ate. Because the ghetto Jews said: "The peel is healthy. In the peel there is iron and under it there is sugar, and that's why cattle are so healthy and strong—because they eat the peel."

KIDDUSH HASHEM

THIS TOOK PLACE in the months of Elul and Tishrei in the year one thousand nine hundred and forty-four.

All the ghettos and labor camps where any Jews were to be found had been liquidated by the Nazis. Only in the ghetto of Lodz there still lived some seventy thousand Jews, worn out by slavery and hunger.

The ghetto was composed of factories, and Jews were put to work manufacturing a variety of merchandise and armaments the Germans needed to carry on the war. The German overseers of the ghetto turned a pretty penny from the labors of their Jewish slaves—so they made every effort to keep the ghetto going for as long as possible. It also helped keep them from having to go the front.

Jews were persuaded by now that they were going to survive the war, having managed to elude so many "selections" and epidemics—and now, just over there, on the banks on the other side of the Vistula, stood the Red Army, and air-raid alarms keep sounding day and night.

In the course of one such alarm that lasted almost three

hours, all work and movement in the ghetto came to a halt. Hundreds of planes flew by coming from the west and flying eastward. Yet not a single anti-aircraft gun went off. The best indication that the Hun no longer had anything to play around with. Beyond the ghetto fence they could see the roads filled with fleeing *Volksdeutschen*—ethnic Germans—carrying their living and inanimate possessions with them.

Long columns of wounded German soldiers could be seen painfully making their way down the road, as well as broken-down vehicles and airplane parts.

Jews read a lesson into what they were seeing: "A bad beginning makes a bad ending."

During the night, one Jew ran to another to spread the good news that the Russians were now on *this* side of the Vistula, and all of Warsaw was occupied.

Ecstatic at the news and filled with suspense, no one was able to get much sleep that night.

The next morning, Jews reported that the Red Army was advancing like an avalanche, and was now in Radom. An hour later it was announced that they had reached Opoczno and Konskie. An hour after that it was reported that the Red Army was already inside Tomaszow Mazowiecki, in Piotrkow Trybunalski and Koluszki.

Engineer Hirsch took out the map he had been keeping hidden someplace or other, spread it out over the table, pointing with his finger for the benefit of those who stood bent over the table crowding round him: "See that, everybody," he drew his finger along the map, "they're on all the roads leading to Lodz. It's just a matter of hours before we're liberated!"

His wife Dvora Leah added: "They're coming by way of the Zgiers road, the Pabianitz, the Konstantin, and the Brzeziny roads."

Old Sompolinski cried aloud: "Well, what did I tell you people? Faith! Jews, have faith! It's even possible that the soldiers at the barbed wire have also retreated and we don't know about it. We ought to send someone out to take a look."

* * *

A provisional central committee was created, representing all the parties and factions. The people must not be left leaderless at a time like this. Quietly and without fuss, they began to organize a militia. Pious Jews prayed for the success of the liberators.

In front of the garment factory a crowd of Jews had gathered. By the wall of the factory stood tables, one on top of the other, and a chair.

The mob had trampled down the bits of radish, beet, and carrot leaves the Jews had planted there to still their hunger, looking forward to the day of their ripening—and now their toil had come to naught. Everyone waited, curious and impatient to discover just what Gauleiter Hans Bübow (accursed be his name and his memory) would say.

Off in a corner, stood engineer Hirsch, his wife Dvora Leah, and both their children. They huddled together with a premonition of something evil.

The German, Hans Bübow, arrived with the Jewish elder Mordecai Chaim Rumkowski. The crowd rocked with sudden fear, as if it had been lashed with a whip. Hans Bübow climbed up on the tables. He struck a pose like an actor about to perform. With an ingratiating little smile he said: "Good morning."

The Jews were taken aback. Hans Bübow, sensing it immediately, continued:

"My dear Jews! I will speak to you as an Elder. My dear sisters and brothers. You have worked faithfully for the *Wehrmacht*. Now, with the Russians approaching, we need your help again to continue the war. Germany is smashed! All Germany lies in ruins!"

The Jews, half-dead, tormented by hunger, beatings, and terror, savored the sweet taste of vengeance.

Bübow raised his voice:

"I am evacuating the factories, the machinery, the goods— everything. Families may remain together. Pack everything away. I am shipping the factories to Vienna: every day I'll transport another factory. In Vienna you will not have to stand in line for soup; you will have your own food to cook. I swear to you there will be nothing lacking in Vienna."

With the tone of one offering sound advice he turned to the Jews again.

"Whoever remains here will be destroyed by Russian bombs. Open your windows at night and you will hear how close the front is. When the Russians come they will kill you all because with your labor you helped us carry on the war against them. Hurry and pack quickly. Let us save ourselves. Remember: there is little time left!"

Gestapo man Hans Bübow saw that the crowd of semi-corpses that encircled him in a dense ring were looking up at him with mistrust, and he began to boil with rage. With his fat, stumpy fists he beat his breast and shouted at them: "What! You don't believe me? If I wanted to kill you, would I be afraid of you? I would drive you all to the cemetery and shoot you down like dogs—you Jewish swine!"

The Jews felt that now he spoke the truth.

"Are you going to pack?" he bellowed.

"Yes!" they answered.

"Are you going to work?"

"Yes!"

"You say 'yes' now, but later you'll change your minds! Will you go willingly?"

"Yes!" the half-dead called out.

"Everyone is going willingly then!" he concluded, and jumped off the table onto the ground.

The "Elder of the Jews," Mordecai Chaim Rumkowski, now crawled up onto the table. The people hoped for a word of comfort from him, but quite placidly he said: "My dear brothers and sisters. The Ghetto is being transferred. Keep together. Entire families must ride together so as not to be separated."

When the two had left the spot, Jews commented on the speeches.

"What's going to happen?" Dvora Leah asked her husband, engineer Hirsch.

And engineer Hirsch replied:

"What do we do?"

"Let be what will be!" old Sompolinski mixed in. "At least we've lived to see their end. If a German can address us as "My dear Jews," "My dear brothers and sisters," then we've lived to see their defeat. Yes, they're as good as buried!" And he stormed off.

In one hand, Dvora Leah carried her three-year old son, Simkhale, and with the other, led her seven-year old daughter, Rivkale. "If we could only hide someplace," she said to her husband. "But. . . ." She was swept along by the fleeing crowd before she could finish. A German had arrived, and the people fled from the square like doves from a hawk.

From the wall, screaming placards announced in three languages: German, Polish, and Yiddish:

TOMORROW GARMENT SHOPS #1 AND #2 WILL BE TRANSFERRED.

ALL WORKERS AT THESE SHOPS ARE TO ASSEMBLE WITH THEIR BAGGAGE AND THEIR FAMILIES AT 8:00 A.M. AT THE MARISHIN- RADAGAST RAILROAD STATION.

Early that morning, hundreds of Jews came to the station with their bundles. They found no one there. They waited for a long time, but no train came. Now they were certain the war was over. Not a German was in sight. They picked up their bundles and went home.

Old Sompolinski ran breathlessly to engineer Hirsch and told him what happened, adding: "If the train isn't running, then all the roads are cut off."

The food administration began to distribute a ration of herring. Jews had not tasted herring since the war broke out. Hirsch smacked his lips: "They say we'll be getting chocolate, rice, white bread and many other good things. These are all good omens. The food was on its way to Germany, but the road has been cut off and the coaches stranded in the ghetto."

"Now the Germans are toadying to us," the young poet Sompolinski philosophized, "we'll be getting the food . . ."

Next morning the Jewish police, carrying identification passes (everyone had a pass with his photograph on it describing his work status. These were kept in the labor office and the Germans used them during their various "selections"), went from house to house picking out the people who were to be "transferred." They picked out several thousand people and took them by streetcar to Marishin-Radagast. The machinery, work-tables, and benches also rode along with them.

Those who were left behind saw a good omen: the factories were retreating! When later the security police arrived (rather than the SS or the Gestapo) they were convinced of it.

Every member of the ghetto administration participated in transferring the ghetto: the ghetto police, the fire brigade, chimney sweeps, porters. All lent a hand, rounding up the Jews like dog-catchers cornering dogs. Twice daily the trains were loaded with five to ten thousand Jews.

Across Polish fields, drowned in golden sunlight, crawled a freight train of more than a hundred cars, each car guarded by SS men with machine-guns.

As the Jews were loaded into the trains they were given a loaf of bread and half a pound of sugar. Ramps, made of wide boards, had been placed at the car openings to make it easier for the people to go up with their bundles. The SS even provided the cars with barrels of water and black coffee. Before boarding, each person was given all the bread and soup he wanted. The Jews recognized only good signs in all this.

Families tried to remain together. No one allowed himself to eat the bread indiscriminately. They thought the trip might take many days and it would be better to ration the provisions.

In one of these cars was engineer Hirsch, his wife Dvora Leah, and the two children. Rivkale was more conspicuous than any of the other children. She had blonde hair and sky-blue eyes. She was lively and curious; always asking questions. About some things she didn't ask, but wanted to see with her own eyes, touch with her own little hands.

Rivkale stood at the window which was criss-crossed with barbed wire, and looked out. She had to stand on her pack to reach the window. She marveled at everything: "Oh, green fields! . . . Oh, pretty cows! . . . Oh, chickens! . . . Oh, such a pretty forest!"

It all seemed to Rivkale like a dream.

Until the fall of 1942 she had been together with her parents at her grandmother's, in the town of Sonick. Before the liquidation of Sonick, her father, engineer Hirsch, had bought himself an assignment in a factory for a huge sum of money, not to mention gold and precious stones. Since he was a radio technician and the Germans could use him, they let him stay together with his wife and children. Later, they were all sent to the ghetto of Lodz.

The sun spread its golden rays over the Polish landscape. This was the golden Polish autumn. The air was filled with the scent of ripe fruit and grain. Rivkale drank deeply of the fragrant air. She became engrossed in the birds she saw flying by. She wanted to be free as they, fly where and when she wanted. She was overcome with a desire to roll in the tall, green grass, stretch out in it, and go to sleep, as she used to do in her grandfather's field in Sonick.

Everyone was pushing to get to the window for a breath of air and a glimpse of the world. The jostling brought Rivkale out of her dream.

One corner of the car was piled high with bread; it lay there unguarded.

"Consider what man is!" the poet Sompolinski declared in amazement. "Only yesterday in the ghetto they hid the little pieces of bread, not only from strangers, but from relatives; but when you're just a little satiated and have a whole bread, then no one is afraid he'll be robbed. Only through hunger did the Germans make us inhuman!"

One corner of the car was fenced off with a sheet and served as a toilet.

In the middle of the car stood two full barrels of water and a pail of black coffee. Everyone who smoked, on entering the train, received a pack of one-hundred cigarettes. (In the ghetto you almost never saw a cigarette).

Even Mordecai Sompolinski saw in this a sign of a favorable change. Just as soon as the SS closed the car, he declared:

"Listen, people, we must organize ourselves here so as to prevent anarchy. The first thing we must do is elect a leader. . . ."

Sompolinski had his entire family in the car with him. Before the war he had had a book of poems published that was warmly received by the critics. In the ghetto he worked in an office, and as a result he looked a bit better than the rest. He buried some of his manuscripts in a cellar in the ghetto, and he was carrying some with him.

Sompolinski's words aroused the confidence of his listeners and he continued:

"We must conserve the water as long as possible. We have no idea how long we are going to be in this car!"

"Right!" a youth called out. "In the year nineteen hundred thirty-nine the Germans dragged me along in a car for seven days and seven nights, and several thousand Jews died of hunger and thirst on that train!"

"I move that Sompolinski be our elder!" someone cried out. Everyone agreed.

"Even though we have two barrelsful of water," Sompolinski went on, "let no one take a drop till tomorrow. The same with the bread. And let's not dirty the car."

He then turned to his younger brother to take a pencil and a sheet of paper and write down the names of every station the train passed through so they would have some idea of where they were being taken. Everything that Sompolonski told them was done.

Sompolinski was of medium height, with light brown hair and an aristocratic face. He wore eyeglasses with dark frames.

Sompolinski's father was much shorter than his son. He unpacked his bag, took out a hammer and knocked some nails into the wall.

"People, take off your clothes and hang them up here."

"My dear sir," a young man said to him, "I see you're a practical man. You've even brought a hammer and nails with you."

"What else, young man?" he retorted. "We may come to a place where such things will come in very handy. In my lifetime I've wandered more than once from town to city, and from city to town. I know the value of little things. Do you remember our condition when we were driven into the ghetto? It's a good thing this time they allowed us to take along as much as 100 pounds of baggage per person."

"I know some Jews who took along their bedding: even clothes and underwear for summer and for winter; furniture, too."

"That shows," engineer Hirsch puts in, "that we're really being sent to work. They need our muscle now. Our baggage is being transported in extra cars. You can see for yourselves, we've even gotten a loaf of bread each, sugar, two barrels of water, and a pail of coffee. On closing the car Bübow asked whether we all got our rations."

A girl wept bitterly. She had not taken any baggage with her. She had prepared a rucksack at home, but she was hiding somewhere else and when the Germans pulled her out, they only allowed her to take along the few things she had with her. And what would she do now? She wants everyone to contribute from their packs to make one up for her. They assure her that once they get their baggage back they will see to it.

"I was opposed to going," Sompolinski's cousin asserted. "I was certain the Russians would liberate us any day. When the police tore up the garrets and cellars, I lay hidden in a shack. I tore the clay off the ceiling and squeezed myself in. I lay there curled up and closed the hole with chunks of clay. No one would have thought you'd find a living being there. But how long can you last without bread and water? And then comes the order: the death penalty for anyone found in the vicinity. After two weeks of this I came out. Perhaps, I thought, we're really being sent to work. It's better to delay one's death as long as possible. Liberation must come *sometime*."

"I tell you people," old Sompolinski cried out, "the Russians will liberate us on our way!"

Engineer Hirsch tells how he, his wife, children, and neighbors hid themselves in a garret. It was so crowded they almost choked. The police ran around with axes and broke down the doors. The house shook to its very foundations. It was a wooden house, with two stories and a pointed roof concealing several rooms in the garret. All around the garret were living quarters— and it was these rooms the police were breaking apart. "We lay at the top, just under the roof. We had pulled the ladder in after us. And just imagine, it didn't even occur to them that a few steps away about twenty adults and children lay hidden. That's how we spent over two terror-stricken weeks!"

Sompolinski's younger brother calls out the stations as he writes down the names. He describes a native German, in civilian clothes and carrying a gun, guarding a small bridge crossing a river into a forest. "He didn't want to go to the front so he bought himself a post," he explains. "At one place in the forest I saw a mass of bayonets. This will be a fighting position...."

"If that's so," Hirsch remarks, "then the further we're away the better."

"If you'd stay here then you'd have a chance of being liberated right away," Sompolinski cut in. "Just imagine, you've lived to see the very moment that the Red Army marches in and the Germans are running away. They throw their weapons away and you cut them to pieces! You have your vengeance! But if they are taking us to the heart of Germany, who knows how long it will be before we're liberated?"

"Bite your tongue!" old Sompolinski shouts at him angrily. "You'll see, we'll be liberated on our way there! The Germans are fleeing like poisoned rats!"

"Papa, you're naïve," his son says, "the Gestapo is spreading these rumors itself through our Sonder.* So that executioner Bübow (may he be damned forever!) is *transporting* the ghetto, is he? He's the one who liquidated all the ghettos around Lodz, shot thousands of Jews with his own hands, is he the one you believe? They said our train goes to Vienna. I don't believe that gangster wants to save us from the bombs! You heard what the SS said: 'The Jews are going voluntarily....' Pray that it turns out well!"

It was the absolute truth. The Germans were always good at spreading hopeful rumors. The "Sonder" firmly believed in them too: and, the Jews argued, if the Sonder say so—"well they got it from the Germans."

A Gestapo officer revealed to a "Sonder" officer the "secret" that the Red Army was already on the outskirts of Lodz. The "Sonder" officer could not keep such wonderful news to himself and immediately told it to his colleagues, and they, to the ordinary police. And with lightning speed the rumor spread throughout

*Jewish Police who worked directly with the Gestapo.

the entire ghetto. After Sompolinksi's pessimistic speech there was silence in the car. Everyone turned to his own thoughts.

The sun set low in the sky and painted it purplish red. The train cut through a forest of leaves. The forest looked as if it were on fire. Rivkale saw it all.

"Oh, the forest is on fire!" she cried out. Her mother, Dvora Leah, pushed her way to the little window. Before her arose a vision of old times in the little town of Sonick: the forest, the river, the wide meadows, the sunset behind the orchard, and the evenings when she used to meet with her future husband without her parents' knowledge. "Isn't it better," she thought, "to look but once upon God's world and die?"

Meanwhile a youth carrying a pot stole over to the barrels of water. Sompolinski's cousin shouted at him, clenching his fists. Sompolinski himself walked over to him and reasoned with him quietly:

"Everyone agreed we weren't to touch the water until tomorrow morning—must you be an exception?"

"Just a tiny bit," he begged.

"If you drink, then everyone else will want to. You had your share today. Who knows how many days we'll be without water? Even tomorrow all we'll get is a little potful, no more!"

Several Jews immediately moved to stand guard over the water. The train sweeps onward, as night descends. The poet Sompolinski looks out the little window and sees that the train is passing through a station lit up by large electric lamps from high steel posts. "I believe," he remarks, "we are now beyond the Polish border. First, the stations are all lit as if there weren't even a war on; and, second, in Poland there aren't any such high electrical steel posts—only wooden ones. Therefore we must be in Germany." He tries to decipher the name of the station, but the train is on the opposite track. He tells his younger brother to try to catch the names of the oncoming stations.

Sompolinski decides that just as soon as the train arrives at its destination, he would stick a letter into one of the cracks of the car so that the next transport of people would know where they were being taken. . . .

"According to all the signs," Hirsch remarks, "it seems we are really being taken to Vienna for work. If not, why should Bübow have sent along all the machinery?"

Suddenly, there was a burst of lightning and thunder. It felt as if the train were tossed up high and would be shattered to pieces. For several seconds everyone was blinded; all experienced their final moment. There was plenty of room in the car now. No one felt hungry or thirsty. The frightening sighing of a young man brought everyone back to consciousness. The young man had broken open the corner window, put his head out searching for a spot to jump. He fell back on top of a group of Jews with a bullet in his jaw, part of his nose torn off. His last words were: "Revenge, Jews!"

"Oh God, let me have the honor of dying in this car," an elderly Jew cried out, "so that I may have a Jewish burial."

The father of the deceased said *Kaddish*, weeping bitterly. Rivkale's heart contracted sharply and she cried with the old man.

Families moved closer together, clutching onto one another.

Dvora Leah embraced her husband and children.

"God, do not separate us. Whatever happens, wherever it happens, let us stay together," she cried out.

Dawn was still breaking, the sky barely blue, and Rivkale was already looking out the window. Some Jews recited their morning prayers; others ate some food. Sompolinski's brother stood with his sheet of paper and pencil, waiting to write down the name of some station.

Everyone was trying to figure out their real destination. Were they really being taken to Vienna for work as the SS said on counting them off on the train?

Suddenly Rivkale cried out:

"Oh, just look! Mommy, look!"

Her mother started up and flew to the window. Outside stretched a double fence of barbed wire upon iron posts. Inside the fence were numerous barracks. On the square, queer people who gave the impression of being mad, moved about. Guardhouses fortified with machine guns stood out prominently.

"Oh, woe is us!" Dvora Leah cried out. "They've fooled us again! Everyone put on your best clothes! They're going to take everything away. Let us at least wear our best clothes."

Dvora Leah began dressing the children in their best clothes and little shoes.

Engineer Hirsch unpacked his winter shoes from his rucksack, also pulling his winter coat on.

The doors of the cars were torn open with wild outcries even before the train came to a standstill.

"All down! Leave everything in the cars! Out! Out! Off! Off!"

Everyone rushed for a loaf of bread. It hurt them to have denied themselves the opportunity of filling up with bread, the only such opportunity they had during all the war years. Meanwhile clubs were cracking over their bodies:

"*Raus*! *Raus*! Out! Out!" They were being beaten by "Canadians"—Jews, old prisoners at Auschwitz who lived through many hells and now (a short spell before being cremated) found themselves in somewhat better circumstances. They wore concentration-camp clothes with blue-white stripes and yellow-red triangular patches (red for political "transgressions"; yellow for Jewish "transgressions"). They wore special numbers on their jackets and trousers. Their left arms were also branded with numbers. These people were now unloading the cars. They were called "Canadians" because they had plenty to eat. The Germans dulled their minds by feeding them opium. They were chasing everyone out of the cars, beating them so that they would leave their things in the cars. Engineer Hirsch and Dvora Leah and the children ran out of the car, just managing to avoid the clubs.

When old Sompolinski came out onto the platform, a young "Canadian" began to beat him, cursing him with a volley of obscenities. The old man saw that the "Canadian" was dead drunk and a Jew, and cried out:

"But you're a Jew! How can one Jew kill another?"

The "Canadian" lowered his eyes. He neither lifted his hand nor his voice again—but when the SS came up, he proceeded with his "work." (They had to strike the people in any case, so they chose their victims from among the old, for these people were among the first to be sent to the crematoria.)

The leader of the "Canadians" shouted an order:

"Women and children are to remain on the square! Men, on the other side! Off! Off!"

The men kissed their wives and children good-bye. The "Canadians" pulled them away. Most of them could not be torn away—and so the clubs worked furiously. Many people were already lying on the platform bloodied and beaten.

The "Canadian" pulled Hirsch away from his wife and children. The children cried fearfully. Dvora Leah held Simkhale and Rivkale in her arms. They stretched their little hands out to their father and wept:

"Daddy! Daddy!"

Hirsch decided that at no cost would he be separated from his family. All four embraced. They looked like a tree with many branches. . . . An SS officer appeared. The "Canadians" knew the family could not escape their fate and they were only endangering themselves by not carrying out orders, and they went at Hirsch with their clubs, breaking him free of his family.

He resisted with all his strength, but it was useless. His wife and children now stood alone, their hands stretched out, pleading to him.

"Have you not God in your heart? How can God witness all this?" the poet Sompolinski asked the leader of the "Canadians."

"God? There's no God here! Maybe there!" he answered,

pointing with his club in the direction of the city. "This is Auschwitz!" he cried out. He was of medium height, with broad shoulders, a brown face, and a black moustache. He was notorious in one of the districts of Lodz as a playboy—they called him "Moishel the Butcher."

"But they've fooled us!" a Jew mourns.

"Fooled you!" Moishel the Butcher apes him. "You should have done anything rather than come here. Here everything goes into the oven. Here, you come in through the door and leave through the chimney."

The Jews understood not a word of what he said.

"My dear Jews, better give everything to me, there they will take it away from you anyway," he continued. "In there . . . you will no longer need anything!"

The Jews, frightened, gave him everything they possessed. A boy handed him his watch. He looked it over, threw it on the ground and crushed it with his heavy boots. He became enraged as he cried:

"Such trash! You're keeping the good things for them?"

Another gave him a banknote (50 German marks) and he tore it to little pieces. "Money has no value here! You can wipe your bottom with it! This is Auschwitz!"

The young "Canadian" who beat old Sompolinski caught sight of his own wife and child on the platform. He ran up to them with outstretched arms. She did not notice him. When he cried out "Hannele" she stretched out her arm and cried back "Leibl,"— they kissed. For several seconds both forgot where they were. The child wept, frightened by his father. Hannele looked at him and for the first time saw that he had become entirely transformed. He looked like a well-stuffed wild animal. Both had tears in their eyes. Hannele thought that whatever the outcome at least she and her child were now safe. The father would care for them. And to think that she had already given him up for dead! Leibl controlled himself. He knew that if she went with the child, both would end up in the crematorium. It would be best to give the child to some older woman. Hannele is still young and has a chance of surviving the war. The Germans need young hands.

Leibl had made it his job to snatch infants away from young mothers and throw them into the arms of elderly women. In this way he could still save some few young lives. This he did when the Germans were not looking. . . . With the speed of lightning he snatched the child from Hannele. "We must make a sacrifice. Perhaps you'll be saved!"

"No!" Hannele cried out. She fought back and the child remained with her.

The SS arrived and a deathly silence fell upon the crowd. An SS officer spoke in a hoarse voice:

"Hear me! You need have no anxiety! You've been brought here for work. Women, children, old people will be taken to a recreation camp! The sick—to a hospital! *You must give in to us quietly!*" he stressed.

Dr. Mengele, a German in an SS uniform, picked out the sick and crippled.

Two prisoners in civilian clothes, with white bands decorated with a Red Cross on their left arms, carried them away on a stretcher, putting them in a Red Cross truck.

Most of the people envied them.

"Do you see," a Jew remarks to his neighbors, "they're taking them straight to the hospital."

"It looks like they'll be lacking nothing here!" another calls out, jealous.

"You see, he's envious already," a third admonishes him. "It's time something good happened to them. Didn't they suffer enough in the ghetto?"

Little Rivkale listened to everything that was happening. She was pale with fright and held on to her mother's dress. She wanted to curl up and disappear. Dvora Leah clutched her tightly while carrying in her other arm little Simkhale. He clasped his mother's neck with his little hands, his head buried in her breast. He sobbed pitifully; every limb cried out: "Protect me! Protect me!"

The father, engineer Hirsch, was on the opposite side among the men. He tried to push his way to his wife and children, but murderous blows drove him back, bloodied and beaten.

"Five in a row!" Moishel the Butcher orders. The "Canadians" force the people into rows with obscenities, curses, and blows. In a few minutes the whole transport is arranged in military formation.

Dr. Mengele arrives in his SS uniform, smoking a cigarette to kill the germs. All the rows march past before him—"selection." He looks everyone in the face, his eyes piercing as knives. He points with his forefinger: some to the right, some to the left. That is, those who are to go directly into the ovens, and those who are to linger awhile in suffering.

Near him stand SS men, rifles and bayonets drawn, guarding that everyone goes to his appointed side.

A short distance off stand groups of SS men watching that none run off from one side to another.

Engineer Hirsch wondered why they needed so many SS men and such an abundance of arms. Who is going to run off? Everyone wants to work! That is why they were brought here. . . .

When Hirsch walked up to Dr. Mengele and the German saw how bloodied Hirsch was, he pointed to the left.

The old, the weak, women with children were all sent to the left side. The young and strong were sent to the right. Sompolinski asked to be allowed to go with his father and Dr. Mengele gave him permission to do so.

When Dvora Leah and her children came up to Dr. Mengele and he saw Rivkale with her sky-blue eyes and blond curls, he thought she looked like an Aryan. He stared at her for several seconds. He smiled at her sarcastically and Rivkale smiled back. He looked Dvora Leah over carefully; also Simkhale who had his little head buried in her breast. Suddenly he decided he would not send them to the crematorium just now. In this way he could show the rest that mothers with children also live in Auschwitz and receive the same ration as those who are productive. Besides, he thought they would present him with an opportunity of gratifying some sadistic whim of his. So he made a motion with a finger—and half-heartedly ordered:

"To the right!"

Meanwhile the young "Canadian" would not leave the place where his wife and child were standing. He arranged it so as it would appear he was keeping order here. They called him "Leibl Fonfatch" (for his speech was nasal because of a hare lip) and he was a street porter by trade.

In the ghetto of Lodz he belonged to the "White Guard"—that is, he was a two-legged horse. He pulled a wagon of flour and was always covered over with white. These porters were an organized group and often helped themselves from the sacks. Once the police caught Leibl taking a bit of flour in order to still the frightful hunger of his wife and child. It came to court. Rumkowski's judgment marked him as a war criminal and he was penalized by being expelled from the ghetto.

He was sent here to Auschwitz to a certain death. But on stepping off the train Dr. Mengele saw at once that Leibl Fonfatch was still quite fit and that his behavior was like that of one who found himself at home in Auschwitz. "Why were you sent here?" he asked him. Leibl gave Dr. Mengele an account of his doing and the court's judgment.

"I am a war criminal" he told him.

Leibl found favor in Dr. Mengele's eyes and he was assigned to the labor force. It didn't take very long before he was transferred to the "Canada" group, forming the reception committee on the train platform. In every transport coming from Lodz he looked out for the "Elder" (Rumkowski). He was looking to avenge himself personally. Strangers he beat; acquaintances he tried to help. He also looked out for his wife and child. An idea now occurred to him. Maybe Dr. Mengele would help his wife and child. He would ask him. . . .

When Mengele approached his wife and child, Leibl braced himself like a soldier taking honor guard and said to the doctor with bated breath:

"Herr Doktor, I beg you. This is my wife and child. . . . Please. . . ."

Dr. Mengele did not let him finish and pointed with his forefinger: "Left!"

"If that's so, Herr Doktor," Leibl said, "I want to go with my wife."

"You may go!" Dr. Mengele answered him.

Leibl went with his wife and child. Except Leibl Fonfatch, no one knew yet where they were going. A huge column of people, five in a row, composed of old men, women, and children was formed. They were heavily guarded by SS men as they marched off to the left, following the field-kitchen staff, their guiding light, whose steaming pots of soup broke one's will.

Those whom Dr. Mengele sent to the "Right" formed another column, five to a row, the women separated from the men.

This second column envied the first: "Soon they will have hot soup."

"We are always ready to think the worst!" the poet Sompolinski said to his neighbor.

"What else? Of course!"

"God is here too!" the old beaten Sompolinski added, walking third in the row. "Let's not worry, everyone. We must have faith!"

In order to give the new prisoners a false sense of security, the Germans built a camp near the station, composed only of the crippled and the lame. When the two columns marched past this camp they saw hundreds of cripples, well-dressed, and giving the impression of happiness and contentment. This settled the minds of the new arrivals. They comforted each other.

"Do you see? And we were ready to believe the worst!"

"It'll be better here than in the ghetto!" someone cried out almost happily.

When the first column entered the camp, an SS officer, standing on a table, addressed them.

"Hear me! You are all very weak people. The old, the mothers with children, all are going to a recuperation camp. You know that? *Jawohl*?"

"*Jawohl!*" all answered.

"But my dears," he continued pleasantly, "you must bathe after such a difficult journey. The clothes must be disinfected. Undress calmly and put your clothes away neatly so they will not get mixed up. The faster the better, for some warm, tasty soup is waiting for you. It will get cold!"

The young "Canadian," Leibl Fonfatch, he alone knew what all this meant, but he didn't want his wife and the others to know that they were being taken directly to the crematories. And so he remained silent. Nevertheless his blood was boiling, thirsting for revenge because of what he saw here and the orders he was forced to carry out. He had done what he was told to do in the hope that he would yet live to see his wife and child. Now, all was lost: his wife and child are to be gassed, and he with them. His conscience tormented him: Why did he have to bloody so many Jews with his own hands before the eyes of the SS, trying to show them how faithful he was? Why hadn't he rather murdered an SS man—at least then he would have had a feeling of revenge and have gone to his death with a calm conscience.

Leibl had a sharp knife in his back pocket which he had "organized" from one of the transports. He seldom used it, yet constantly sharpened it so that it would not grow dull. No one was to know of this knife. The penalty was death. This was considered by the Germans as "possessing arms." When he first held the knife in his hand he recalled how he had driven away more than one scoundrel who came around Pepper Street to kill Jews. Perhaps he would have need of such a knife again.

Leibl watched the Jews taking off their clothes. His wife had already undressed the child, and was now beginning to undress herself. The orderlies and an SS officer went about inspecting whether everyone was undressing. When the SS officer came to Leibl and saw that he was still completely clothed, he asked angrily: "Why don't you undress, you swine?"

An age-old rage that had been repressed all this time in Leibl surfaced. Swiftly, he drew his knife. With one hand he pushed back the officer's head and with the other he slit his throat. It happened so quickly that before the officer could draw his revolver, blood was already spurting from his throat. Soon hundreds of SS men came running and shot into the crowd. Hundreds of women, men, and children fell under the fire.

The firing lasted exactly five minutes. The commandant kept time. The Germans did not make an investigation. The dead SS officer was immediately removed.

After killing the officer, Leibl took his wife and child and crept up to the door of the gas chamber, escaping the fire.

Those who were shot remained lying on the mounds of clothes, soaking in their blood. A great many were still groaning, but they were soon dragged to the crematory.

The door was opened and Leibl, together with his wife and child, were the first to enter. Everyone received a white towel and a green piece of soap, stamped with the letters R.J.F. (for *Rein Juden Fetts*, "Pure Jew-Fat").* The Germans, using flashlights, inspected the mouth, the nose, and rectum of each prisoner.

---

*The belief that Jewish victims were rendered into soap was common both during and after the Second World War. Leading scholars of the Holocaust have found no evidence that the Nazis used human fat to manufacture soap.

They were searching for gold and diamonds. Whoever had gold teeth was marked with India ink. The gold teeth of such people were extracted before they were cremated.

Leibl held his wife's and child's hands and approached his death courageously. But he could not forget how old Sompolinski, whom he had beaten earlier, had asked him: "How can one Jew beat another?" Leibl's heart felt as if it were being cut into pieces. The questioning eyes of old Sompolinski followed him everywhere. Leibl told his wife that here she would not have to work as hard as in the ghetto; that there was more food here than in the ghetto. He's an old resident here and would help her. It would be easier for her than for the others. Leibl recognized a familiar voice as he heard: "Well, engineer Hirsch, we've met again, both bloodied and both on our way together?"

"We're still on the same chapter, father," his son, the poet, added with a touch of sadness in his voice.

Leibl turned around and saw the elderly Jew whom he had struck. He turned back quickly so that their eyes would not meet. He could not wait to get into the gas chamber.

"Yes, Mr. Sompolinski," Hirsch sighed. "You said you were certain the Russians would free us on the way? Where is Russia? America? And where is God? God? . . ."

It was a high-ceilinged hall; the walls were lacquered with decorations of young banana trees. On all sides hung carved mirrors. There were also cupboards and long benches like those in a ritual bathhouse.

"Let us just survive this bath," old Sompolinski consoled Hirsch, "and we'll be all right. Have faith!"

An iron door opened and disclosed a long, low room with a wet declining floor. The piercing sound of a whistle threw everyone into a fright.

An SS officer politely ordered everyone to leave his towel here. After the bath they would be returned to them. They must hurry, for the showers are getting cold.

He divided the people into groups of five and called out continuously:

"Next, please!"

Leibl went in first. He led his wife and child by the hand. When the room was packed full, they closed the iron door. In the middle of the room were four-cornered iron pipes with little holes like a sieve, from which the gas seeped out.

Outside, another party from the transport waited its turn in this "bath."

The column of women and column of men which Dr. Mengele sent to the right were directed to another part of Auschwitz-Birkenau. Here stood a one-story, red-brick building which looked like a factory. This was the bathhouse.

The women were first to enter.

Outside, on the sand, among the thousands of young women who waited their turn, lay Dvora Leah with her two children. The mothers from whom their children were snatched away looked on enviously. The children, still pale from fright, clung to their mother.

Some of the other women attended to their children too; those who still had pieces of bread shared it with the children.

Rivkale suffered from thirst and constantly cried out for water.

It was past midday.

Four of the girls who had been in Auschwitz for some time and now were employed in the kitchen, stole pails of water and distributed drops of it among the people. The girls tried to comfort the women. They told them they were from Cracow and that the worst was over. There was no need to worry; the war couldn't last much longer anymore.

A boy of about fifteen, dressed in a concentration camp uniform (a white-blue striped outfit with a red patch and a number on the left breast) and carrying a large metal box, ran up to the women. Like a newsboy calling out the latest news, he shouted: "Sluts, whores, charity saves from death! Give gold! Money! Diamonds! Give all you've got! Charity saves from death!"

They gave him whatever they had with them.

The women asked him where they were being taken and he told them: "To camp H!" That is, directly to Heaven.

When no one understood the irony he shouted again: "Another menagerie!" and ran off with his box full of jewelry.

Across the fence, not far from where the women were sitting, was a camp full of hundreds of deformed prisoners.

The food which the Germans took away from the Jewish transports was sent to this camp. But it was too much for them to consume, so the Germans allowed them to throw some of it over the fence to the starving women.

When the young "Canadian" left with the box, the cripples began to throw some chunks of cake and bread to the other prisoners.

The starved women scrambled for the food, tearing pieces from each other's hands.

Dvora Leah ran up with both her children. A cripple noticed her, called her to him and tossed her half a cake.

Dvora Leah thanked him. She observed the people, listened to their talk and was amazed to discover that not a single Jew was among them. They were all Poles. They wore civilian clothes and looked rested.

"You see, we worried for nothing," she said to her neighbor. "If such cripples are treated well, what have we, healthy ones, to worry about?"

"We'll be better off here than in the ghetto," her neighbor answered. "We will work; the women with children, the old and weak will be sent to a recuperation camp. They will lack nothing there either!"

"Certainly! Certainly!" the others agreed.

*   *   *

When the sun had set, they finally sent the exhausted women to their bath.

Inside was a large hall of over 100 yards in length and width.

Large bundles of clothes were piled high at the sides. The sound of a whistle threw them into a deathly silence.

"All undress!" came a voice thundering.

"Have the men leave!" the women begged and were answered with a volley of rubber clubs.

"You're not at home now! This is Auschwitz!"

The women quickly threw off their outer garments and remained standing in their underclothes.

So they were beaten again with even more terrifying blows of the rubber clubs. Unwillingly they took off their underclothes as well. With one hand they covered their breasts and with the other their genitals. Out of shame they could not face each other.

A girl helped Dvora Leah undress the children. Dvora Leah was badly shaken, for the SS man who searched her recognized a strong protest in her eyes and beat her. She thought it would be better to die rather than give in to those who lower human dignity. But soon she remembered her two children and it was for them that she must live. She knew that she was human and he was the beast, and when the SS officer met her glance he noticed that she was looking scornfully at him as if she were saying: Humanity will yet triumph over you!

He struck her with his club and abusively ordered her to remove her hands from her breast and genitals.

He looked her over carefully and asked her whether she was pregnant. He examined her stomach. With a flashlight he looked into her mouth, ears and nose. Then he led her to a table, told her to climb up (so that he would not have to bend down) and with fury he parted her legs. Dvora Leah fell unconscious. With the help of his electric flashlight he looked into her vagina, as he thundered with wild abuse. "You whore! You've swallowed the jewelry!" Dvora Leah, still unconscious, was taken off the table.

All the women went through this procedure. Those who were pregnant were immediately sent to the gas chamber.

They drove the women into another, smaller room. Here their heads were shaven. They placed the women in a line, made them walk with their arms raised past two women attendants who shaved off the hair from underneath their arms. One shaved the left armpit; the other, the right.

Dvora Leah held Simkhale with one arm and with the other led Rivkale. All three were shaved. Dvora Leah saw that the women attendants were Jewish. She spoke a few words with them and discovered that Jews from all over Europe were brought here. "What sort of work is there in this camp?" she asked one of them.

"We have a heaven shift and others," the attendant answered.

Dvora Leah did not understand.

On entering the third room Dvora Leah was struck by an SS woman who wielded a long rubber strap. Trying to avoid the blows, she fell onto a long bench around which sat SS men. The woman were forced to climb onto the bench so that the SS wouldn't need to bend down to shave the hair from the women's sex organs.

When Dvora Leah realized what was to come, she wanted to run back, but at the end of the bench stood the SS woman with her rubber strap. Dvora Leah ran up to her children to shield them from the blows. The SS woman shouted at Dvora Leah that if she did not get back on the bench she would kill her on the spot together with her two "damned pups." Dvora Leah, remembering her children, did as she was ordered.

The SS man laughed and joked as he quickly shaved Dvora Leah with a dull razor. He went about it as if he were scraping a hide.

Dvora Leah held herself back from crying out with her last bit of strength.

When she and her children finally escaped to the nearest room, she received such a strong blow on the shoulders that she was forced to double up. This was all a premeditated bit of SS strategy: in this way they could look into the rectum to see whether the prisoners had any currency or jewelry hidden there.

When everyone had passed through all the corridors, a "Canadian" opened a door and gave a prolonged blow on a whistle. The clamor and clatter of a few minutes ago gave way to a frightening silence.

The "Canadian" made a sign with his stick and the women were driven, like animals, into the bath.

Dvora Leah carried both her children so that they would not be lost or trampled underfoot.

The bath was in a large, high hall, without windows. There were many shower-heads but, as it worked out, about twenty people had to stand beneath one shower. The narrowness and noise was unbearable.

There was another prolonged blow of a whistle and a deathly silence descended upon the group.

Suddenly some cold water spurted out. The people started back shouting:

"Oh, cold! Cold!"

The whistle blew again and the silence returned.

This was repeated several times.

Dvora Leah was still carrying the children. She could not put them down for fear they would be crushed. The cold water had thrown an even more terrible fright into them and they began to weep piteously. But the whistle quiets them also; only for a moment though. Soon they break out in an even more bitter weeping.

Suddenly the shower stops and everyone pushes to the door. They want to put some clothes on, for the cold is frightening. But the "Canadians" drive them back with clubs and rubber straps to a distant room. While running from the welter of clubs they receive a rag, taken from a large pile.

The manner of distribution was all planned: the tall are given short dresses; the short, long dresses. These clothes were put together from pieces of old, queerly colored rags.

They were given no shoes, no stockings, and no underwear. Rivkale and Simkhale received the same things as the rest. Then everyone was painted either with a yellow or a red cross on the back, the signs for "Jew-Criminal" and "Political-Criminal." The children were marked in the same way.

When the women left the bath it was already dark, and an autumn wind cut at their wet bodies. They were now at the other side of the camp. The place they had vacated was filled with a second party (all males) ready for the bath.

Dvora Leah observed the women: heads shaven, unshod, covered in rags of queer colors. Even their voices had changed. They had the appearance of inmates at an insane asylum. A mother did not recognize her daughter; a girl her sister. They held hands so as not to lose each other. Dvora Leah looked at her children and saw that they too had become completely transformed.

Now a group of SS women arrived and took command.

"Five in a row!" the order came shouting.

Soon the entire company of women was standing in military formation. The SS leader counted the women and then ordered them to march off.

The column marched on a path which was fenced off with electrified wiring. In one row of fives marched two women and Dvora Leah and her children. She led Rivkale by the hand and carried Simkhale. He curled himself up against her breasts and trembled. He was afraid to look at these strange people. Whenever he glanced at someone he broke into tears.

After marching for half an hour the column of women came to Camp "C." Here they were left standing until midnight.

Finally room was made for them by concentrating three barracks into two. They drove the women into the empty barracks like a herd of cattle.

The barracks was a long, wooden one. In the middle, stretching down the entire length of the room, stood a brick oven of over a yard high and two yards wide. It separated the barracks into two parts. In winter they occasionally lit the oven so as to remind the prisoners that the secret of fire had not been lost. Even then the small flame was not meant to warm the body. The prisoners were only allowed to look at the fire; to come close to the oven, to put one's hands on the bricks was prohibited and punishable. Between the spars of the roof hung boards which proclaimed:

"Work makes life sweet!"

"Keep order!"

"Don't break regulations!"

"Work liberates!"

Dull electric lamps shone down from the ceiling. On both walls, just below the roof, little windows opened to the outside. At the main entrance was the corridor which branched off into two other rooms: one belonged to the "block elder" or barracks chief; the other served as the food magazine. The bit of food for the prisoners was stored here for several hours before it was distributed.

On being herded in, there was a shoving and pushing as everyone scrambled to secure a little sleeping space. Suddenly a whistle blew and fear and silence seized them all.

When the whistle blew again, the silence became even deadlier. All eyes turned in the direction of the ominous sound.

In a corner of the brick oven stood the "block elder,"—a young woman, elegantly dressed, with a head of curly blonde hair. When she saw that all eyes were turned to her, she gave an even stronger blast on the whistle.

Now fear reached an unprecedented height. Death appeared

before their eyes. She raised her stick and drove it down as she shouted: "Everyone to the other side!"

The exhausted women barely managed to crawl over the oven. Dvorah Leah with the children were the last to crawl over on all fours. Simkhale meowed like a sick little cat.

Then came another blast of the whistle and another shouted order: "Everyone back to the other side!"

This was repeated several times.

When the women were already falling over each other, the barracks chief—Fräulein Pollack was her name—shouted:

"I speak to you in plain Yiddish! This is Auschwitz! This is not the ghetto of Lodz where you can buy a loaf of bread for a thousand marks. Whoever has gold, diamonds, pounds, dollars, had better let me have it immediately. Tomorrow morning they will search you with special photographic equipment and if they find anything on you, then it'll be the end of you *all*. Here all are answerable for one! This is Auschwitz. This is where they put an end to people. Thousands in an hour! Outside, behind the wall, you'll find a gallows! They hang hundreds in a day here! I warn you: hand everything over to me before I count ten.

"One! Two! Three!... Ten!...

"Well? No one wants to?...

"Maybe you're afraid to do it openly? You may throw it down on the floor! I know who has things! For the last time—throw it down!"

"Well, give it up then, whoever's got something!" the women shouted at one another.

"All over to the other side!" Fräulein Pollack shouted out again.

When the women were on the other side, the barracks chief, together with her assistant, searched the entire floor with a flashlight. When she found nothing, she cried out:

"Do those few who are holding out on me want to have all the rest hanged on their account? Give it up so we'll get on with the food! Warm soup is waiting for you! Why don't you give it up!"

Dvora Leah, carrying Simkhale in one arm and holding onto Rivkale with the other, was leaning against strange bodies. She could no longer support herself.

Rivkale, who was standing high up on the oven and could see the barracks chief, suddenly called out to her:

"We have nothing!"

Fräulein Pollack turned to her, their eyes met, but the child kept on:

"At the train they took everything from us! At the bath they left us naked and took everything from us! How can we have anything left? . . . We have nothing! . . . Nothing! . . ."

Finally the order came to go to sleep.

One-thousand-three-hundred women are forced to remain in the one barracks on the bare stone floor. There must be total silence; even a whisper means breaking regulations. One's limbs are crushed by strange bodies. People sigh with pain. There isn't room to lie down, so they sit with their legs pushed back and knees up high. Between one's knees another person sits squeezed in. No one wants to sit in such a position, so the "house attendant" goes about striking everyone until they are all seated. This is accomplished in a few minutes.

Near Dvora Leah sat a neighbor of hers. They lived next door to each other in their native town. The woman gave birth to her first child in her eighth year of marriage—three months before coming to Auschwitz. She wouldn't give her little one up, so the German snatched the child from arms. She was beaten back when she tried to join it on the "left" side. Now the milk surged up in her breasts, seeking release. "I see my child being torn by hunger, looking for the breast with his little mouth," she said, imitating the child searching the breast with his little mouth. Suddenly she burst out: "Murderers, give me back my child!"

The house attendant, together with the other barracks

administrators, came running into the room. They beat the woman and those who sat squeezed in near her.

Simkhale, who suffered from thirst and hunger, sucked the milk from the woman's breasts. The woman continued to cry: "I don't want to live!"

Dvora Leah tore a piece from her dress and bound the woman's hand to hers so that she would not be able to throw herself against the electrified wire fence during the night.

It was a night of torture and insanity. All wanted to sleep, but there was no room for them. Everyone regarded his neighbor as a stone thrown in his path. The density of the air stopped one's breath. They were aroused to madness and beat themselves to the point of bleeding. Amid the moaning and cursing, the barracks administration kept on teaching the people the meaning of discipline with their rubber sticks.

Friends took pity on Dvora Leah and her children. They saw that this little family would either be crushed or stifled. They wanted to stand and make room for them, but this was considered "breaking the regulations."

At last nature triumphed and they all fell asleep.

It was like a mighty room of corpses, one thrown upon another.

In one corner of the barracks, a lamp (like the "eternal light" in the synagogue) covered with black blotting paper (as an air raid precaution) cast a dim light upon the sleeping multitude. This was their fortunate moment. Sleep covers all. If they could only sleep until the war's end!

Four o'clock in the morning a long blast of a whistle pierced the stillness.

"Rise! Dress!" came the order.

These house attendants ran about with their sticks. No one wanted to rise. The warmth was comforting and they were weighed down, heavy with sleep.

"Out! Out!" the house attendants and barracks administrators shout as they swing their sticks over the heads of the disordered piles of living corpses.

"Don't shout and beat us so; we are human too!" Dvora Leah begged.

"Human? You are worse than animals. Do animals have to be provided with board and room? You're filth! Out! Out! Faster! Faster!"

The prisoners from all the barracks are forced outside. It is sill dark. A starry sky and a full moon shine down on them. The roofs of the barracks gleam with frost. These are nights of penance. Exhausted, naked, and unshod, they tremble with cold.

Hundreds pack the washrooms that are housed in two separate barracks. The washrooms serve the whole of Camp "C." Not all of them can get in, for there are twenty-eight thousand women prisoners in 32 barracks in Camp "C." A lime path divides the camp in two; 16 barracks on one side, 16 on the other.

One barracks serves as the office; in another live the "Canadians." They come there only to sleep, for they are privileged and are allowed to "work." One barracks serves as the prisoners' clothes magazine. Whenever a transport of people is sent out for work their clothes are supplied from this magazine.

Another barracks is the bath. The transport of people is always washed before it is shipped out for work.

There is always a barracks serving as a toilet, and one as a hospital.

The thousands of women stand outside and begin to form into "ovens" by standing back to back in series of circles.

Dvora Leah and the children are placed in the center where it is warmer. The entire group begins to rock. They rock until those in the center have worked their way back to the periphery, and those at the periphery to the center. Occasionally the group falls apart and so they form another and again place the weaker members together with mothers and children at the center.

Day begins to break.

They joke about their suffering, tell stories and assure each other that the war cannot last much longer.

Yesterday's air-raid alarm was a real "shofar-sound of deliverance"! Dvora Leah exclaims. "The shofar is sounded every day now. This must be the sound of the Messiah's coming!"

"They say that several hundred American 'white doves' flew over the Russian front," a woman declares hopefully. "They carried 'pears' and 'dumplings.' It won't be long before it hails and thunders in Germany."

"They are getting all ten plagues now!" the well-educated Dvora Leah recounts. "Blood, gnats, boils, the Pestilence—yes, they are being wiped out. The lice are devouring them and their blood is not only spilling at the front, but at home too. Hail? Yes, they're getting that too. In Hamburg not a first-born is left. Darkness? It has been dark for them since the first day they began the war. Now they've reached the tenth plague: one leader is killing the other. No need to worry, my sister, we'll outlive 'him'!"

"Let them just give us that piece of bread and soup," a woman shouts. "You don't have to work here, so we'll be better off than in the ghetto of Lodz. The war can't last forever. It must end any day now. I tell you—they're finished!"

A woman brought a bit of black, warm water (so-called coffee) for Dvora Leah and the children. Dvora Leah looked into the bowl, saw her reflection, and did not recognize herself. She had become entirely transfigured. Her shaven head was white as snow. (She used to have long, thick black hair.) She gave a heavy sigh, and divided the bit of warm water among the children. Dvora Leah thanked the woman and asked her where she got it. Of course, she paid for it with several blows.

A sudden ringing of a bell frightens everyone.

"*Appell! Appell! Antreten!*" ("Roll call! Roll call! Fall in!") is heard over the entire camp.

The women run to their places behind the barracks.

The house attendant arranges the women in military formations of five rows. They count the women to see whether their accounts tally. Everyone must stand straight as a stick or be victimized by the sadistic attendants. These attendants also drag the sick and stricken from the barracks and lay them down beside the rows of standing people. They, too, are counted.

The house attendant counts the rows and they do not tally: some "figures" are missing. It happened quite often that women from Dvora Leah's barracks ran away to other barracks, for the barracks chief here was very cruel. At each counting, the house attendant catches women from the other barracks and keeps them until after the count. Sometimes they catch too many and have to drive the extra ones away. This doesn't happen very often though. Usually, no matter how many they catch, some are still missing. After the count, the house attendant drives these captured women away, warning them never to come near the barracks again, that if they do, they will be beaten to death. The house attendants and administrators (the *Kapos*) thus manage to keep the bread rations for themselves. The SS apportions rations of bread according to the numbers in each barracks. Those who are caught are left without bread. With these stolen rations, the house attendants and *Kapos* buy themselves whiskey and cigarettes. Sometimes they even kill prisoners to get their bread rations. The more they kill, the more bread they secure for themselves, and thus the more whiskey and cigarettes.

When the house attendant discovers she needs one more "figure," she walks out onto the path and looks about her for someone to catch. There's no one in sight. The women can hardly stand upright any longer; some have already fainted. The house attendant becomes furious. She runs to the other barracks, but everywhere else the numbers agree. Dvora Leah is afraid she is about to drop to the ground too. Her feet will not hold her any longer. At last a *Kapo* brings in a prisoner whom she has kidnapped from a transport which was about to leave for work. The poor woman thought she would have an opportunity of leaving Auschwitz, when this *Kapo* intervened and destroyed her hopes. The woman begs to be allowed to go. She shows her the number with which she was already branded. Her pleading comes to naught.

In a few moments the camp superintendent, Irma Greiser, arrives. She walks past the rows of women—without a word, only her eyes counting by fives. When she comes to Dvora Leah she sees only three women and a little girl, and she halts. "There's one *figure* missing!"

Dvora Leah opens the top of her dress and shows her the missing "figure"—Simkhale—lying at her breasts, warming himself. The child cries out with a voice of a sick kitten, and then is struck dumb. He is afraid to look at the people. Whenever he sees anyone, he breaks into tears as if he has come face to face with a wild beast.

Irma Greiser gives the child an angry glance and moves off.

With this, the morning roll call ends.

After the roll call, a brass band began to play some lively music. Groups of workers carrying shovels moved to the rhythm of the music as they went to work digging foxholes. Dvora Leah and the rest of the women envied them. To the noise of another band, SS men with dogs chased naked women to the gas chamber. The women's cries were drowned out by the lively marches the band was playing. Neither Dvora Leah nor the other women knew where these naked creatures were being driven.

Dvora Leah and the children sat down against the barracks wall and warmed themselves in the sun.

Many others were also sunning themselves, talking about food and when they would be liberated.

A woman *Kapo*, well-fed and rested, arrived. She carried a club in her hand and on her left arm wore a yellow band on which was inscribed the word *Kapo*. She looked the women over, searching for a victim. She picked out one and began making sport with her. The woman could not keep up with her. The *Kapo* laughed heartily, enjoying every minute of it. The *Kapo* ordered her to stand straight and slowly let herself down to the ground. The poor woman could not manage it and her assailant laughed even more heartily. The *Kapo* now told her to sit down with her feet close together and thus to jump and dance—not on the ground but in the air. The woman tried to do it with all her might, but finally fell to the ground. The *Kapo*'s laughter knew no bounds. This was so comical, the others began to laugh too. When the *Kapo* recovered, she instructed the woman to stretch her arms out and let them down slowly. The woman tried to do it, but her arms wouldn't lift. The *Kapo* told her to look at the flames shooting out of the ovens of the crematory. This meant that she would be among the first to be sent there.

"What is that?" the *Kapo* asked her.

"A bakery," she answered.

"What are they doing there now?"

"They're baking bread; the kind we eat."

The *Kapo* shook her head pityingly.

"What does the word *Kapo* mean?" Dvora Leah asked her.

"*Kapo* means *Kamerad-Polizei*," she answered.

"A fine piece of irony," Dvora Leah thought, "the SS pick out prostitutes from the underworld, turn them into sadists and call them *Kamerad-Polizei*."

The *Kapo*, seeing that prisoners were becoming "chummy" with her, lifted her stick and struck the air as she shouted:

"You slime! You're all going to the ovens!"

When the *Kapo* left, a house attendant came up and asked the group of women whether they were from her native city of Lodz, and did they know her family.

"What sort of work are we going to do here?" Dvora Leah asked her.

"No one works here; here you go directly to the ovens," the house attendant answered indifferently.

The women looked at her.

"Why do you tease us?" one of them asked her. "Do you think you'll frighten us with these terrifying fantasies? We have gone through enough."

"Ha-ha-ha," she answered back, but there was no one to laugh with. "You've gone through enough! You're suffering now? This is paradise! When I came here we slept on nails. The boards of our bunks were hammered with nails and we had to sleep on these every night. Our bodies became like graters; blood poured from us and our wounds became infected. And food? The boiling soup was poured into our hands. The best have been sent to work. They may survive the war. When you leave this place, you leave death and hunger!"

The women were all from a new transport and didn't understand what this native of Auschwitz was telling them. They thought she was making sport of them since they were newcomers.

"If they wanted to kill us, they wouldn't give us such thick soup. We eat better here than in the ghetto of Lodz!" one of them told her.

"Fool! Does it cost them anything? The food is taken from the transports and belongs to you anyway. Here all the Jews are gassed, cremated!"

"I don't believe it! Are we criminals? And how can one human do this to another? All of you are making fun of us!"

"Our misfortune is not to have been murderers, but humanists filled with the spirit of the prophets. That is why we cannot even grasp it. In this world our parents should have brought us up as murderers. Then it would have been different."

"We Jews, because we are filled with the spirit of the prophets, have outlived nations whose power lay in murdering," Dvora Leah cut in. "The sword will be broken and the spirit of the prophets will triumph! Paris has fallen and the invasion has begun. The Red Army is at the Vistula. . . ."

"No one wants to save Jews: neither Russia, nor America, nor England," the house attendant broke in. "What do a few bombs mean to them? A few bombs to blow up the gas chambers and crematories, to put an end to Auschwitz? They know where Auschwitz is and what it is! History will straighten its account with them too! And our brothers in America? Are they doing anything to save us?"

"We may be liberated any minute now!" Dvora Leah put in sharply.

The other women nodded, agreeing. The house attendant shrugged her shoulders. "A real menagerie!" she shouted out and left.

On the road, women with their concealed weapons (pots) were roaming about, looking for prey. Every barracks in the camp sent out its carriers and guards to bring the barrels of soup from the kitchen. The guards beat these "thieves" until they were almost dead. These thieving women hit upon another plan: they would go out as a group and in the ensuing struggle several of them would manage to fill their pots with soup. They would divide the spoils of war among themselves afterwards.

Dvora Leah looked at this spectacle and her heart grew heavy:

"What will be the end?" she sighed. "What will happen to my little ones? What will become of all of us?"

The whole barracks stood in line, waiting for the bit of soup. Dvora Leah felt faint from hunger, and her eyes were dazed. It's twelve o'clock already and they have been outside since four o'clock in the morning and have had nothing to eat yet.

At last they distributed the soup from the barrels, pouring it into old, battered, rusty plates, salvaged from garbage—20 to 30 plates for 1300 prisoners. There were no spoons, for these were forbidden. The soup was boiling and every drop was precious to these starving women. They cleaned the plates with their fingers, licking them off with their tongues. After tasting a bit of food, hunger tormented them even more fiercely. They tore the plates from each other's mouths. "You've gorged yourself enough!" they cried at one another.

The house attendant went about with her club, keeping order.

Dvora Leah and the children stood last in line. Dvora Leah thought she would never get to the soup. One neighbor took pity on her and begged the house attendant to let the mother with the children have their soup first. "We are in Auschwitz," she said "but we must not forget we are still human. How many children have we here in all?"

The house attendant took Dvora Leah and the children out of the line. "Don't think I'm entirely inhuman, even though I am a house attendant," she told her and led Dvora Leah to the barrel of soup and ordered three soups for her and the children.

Dvora Leah said that in the meantime she would take only one soup. When she and the children will have finished this, she'd take the others. She did this for three reasons:

First of all, there were few plates and the hungry women were waiting impatiently for their turn. Then, too, the soup would get cold were she to take all three at once. Thirdly, who could prevent some starved person from snatching a plate of soup from her and running off with it?

Dvora Leah searched the entire camp for a piece of wood to make a spoon. With great effort, she managed to find a thin little splinter of wood. No prisoner was allowed to possess anything outside the rag she received after the bath. The entire camp was cleared of every piece of string, paper, and wood. Dvora Leah washed this piece of wood and ate her soup with it and fed the children with it as well. Of the three plates of soup,

Dvora Leah did not take her whole share; she gave the children most of her portion too.

Dusk. Again the roll call. The women stood for hours. The house attendants and *Kapos* kept order with their clubs.

After the count the rows of women were moved into the barracks. Everyone tried to get in as quickly as possible. On entering, they usually received a small portion of bread and something extra: either a piece of horsemeat sausage, or a bit of synthetic honey, or a bit of margarine. Today they expected to receive an entire loaf of bread for three people (so the administration had announced). There was general rejoicing and everyone wanted to get into the barracks to share in the celebration. Dvora Leah planned to hide one portion for the morning, so that the children wouldn't have to fast until soup-time. She told Rivkale today she would have a larger portion of bread and that tomorrow morning she would also have a piece of bread.

Dvora Leah thought this was a sign the war was coming to an end and the Germans were trying to ingratiate themselves in the eyes of the prisoners. Just think—more bread!

But when Dvora Leah entered the barracks corridor they handed her only quarter-portions. She sat down on the floor, her children beside her, and all three ate up their portions. Now they felt an even greater yearning for food.

Instead of apportioning the bread as announced, the house attendants, *Kapos*, and barracks chiefs kept the extra rations for themselves. With this bread they bought themselves cigarettes, whiskey, matches, meat, milk, and clothes.

Rivkale always asked to be told stories. While Simkhale lay dreaming in her arms, Dvora Leah told her stories of great bowls of soup, large loaves of bread, huge plates of potatoes, warm clothes, and a warm bed to sleep in. Rivkale was enraptured by these decriptions. "Every mealtime will be a celebration," Dvora

Leah declared. "Daddy will sit at the head of the table, near him Rivkale and Simkhale...."

A tumult in the barracks interrupted their dreams. The assistant barracks chief ran about shouting: "Philetzka Genia! Philetzka Genia!" A frightened girl stood up.

"Come over here!" the command came thundering. Philetzka went up, her sister following.

"You said we didn't distribute one bread to three people; only one to *four*! Answer; you slut!"

Philetzka trembled all over from fear. Her tongue wouldn't move. Her teeth chattered audibly.

"Well! Why are you silent, you bitch! Why are you spreading such lies!"

Only after getting a fierce blow on the back could the girl stammer out:

"I didn't say it!"

"You did, you whore! Twenty-five lashes on the ass for you!"

The girl's sister, weeping desperately, ran up to the assistant chief, kissed her hands, and begged: "Don't beat her. She didn't say it. She's ill. She won't survive this. Beat me instead. I'm healthy; give me the lashes!"

Her cries echoed through the barracks.

"No!" the assistant shouted. "Away!"

The house attendant brought a bench and the assistant put the girl on it. She pushed back her dress and warned her not to shout lest she get double the amount. The house attendant held the girl down. The girl was silent, but her sister wept. With every blow of the knotted whip, the girl's sister sighed as if the whip had fallen upon her own body. Dvora Leah and the children didn't have the strength to look. Tears flowed from Dvora Leah's and Rivkale's eyes.

Dvora Leah and the children ran outside. Here they saw a group of children, all under fourteen, demonstrating. The children held their quarter-rations of bread and scraps of synthetic honey stretched out in their little hands and marched through the camp to the administration building. They wanted to show the officer in charge how they were being cheated by the barracks chiefs. The administration building was closed and they stood waiting a long time for the SS officer.

Dvora Leah and the other adults were astounded at the unity and perseverance displayed by the children. Neither a house attendant nor a *Kapo* could stop them. Dvora Leah observed that this children's hunger strike awoke a tremor in the hearts of the camp guards.

Dvora Leah heard that only in one barracks was the bread distributed fairly. Here the prisoners divided the bread among themselves. The whole camp envied them. They also had better soup. Many prisoners tried to join this group. The Germans called them the "building battalion," for they were being assigned to construction work in Germany. The others were certain these people would be among the first to be liberated from Auschwitz.

Dvora Leah began to make plans to smuggle herself into this barracks. They were all mistaken. This group was the first to go to the gas chamber.

The camp chief, Fräulein Irma Greiser, the crown of the Hitler Youth, began bringing Rivkale pretty clothes. She even played with her. Nevertheless, after each meeting, Rivkale's body was covered with black and blue bruises. This happened at the beginning of their acquaintance; later on she only teased her, played with her like a cat and a mouse. It got to the point that whenever Rivkale saw her coming she ran away and hid.

And so the tall Irma Greiser, this daughter of the "master race," came with her hunting dog. The dog knew how to find Rivkale.

Every day Rivkale hides under another porch and every day the dog drags her out by the feet. Rivkale receives more than one blow from Fräulein Pollack, the barracks chief, for hiding, but it doesn't matter. Irma Greiser comes to see Rivkale every after-noon, and Rivkale hides just the same.

When Rivkale is caught, Fräulein Irma Greiser takes her for a walk. She holds her little hand and asks her questions. Rivkale tells her about the ghetto, the hunger, and the frightful journey in the train coming here. One day Rivkale became thoughtful and asked Irma Greiser: "Where is my daddy? We came here together." Irma turned Rivkale's face toward the flaming fires rising from the four red chimneys, like from a smelting furnace.

"Do you see that fire? What is it?" Irma Greiser asked.

Rivkale held back for a moment and then answered: "That's a bakery! They're baking bread now."

Fräulein Irma Greiser broke out in a loud laughter. "Your father is burning there, silly child. Your mother and your brother will burn there also. You as well! The flames will then shoot up that way too."

While Irma was talking, Rivkale played with the leather belt which Irma Greiser always carried with her. On the wide metal buckle, she read out: "God with us."

Suddenly she broke out crying: "If you believe in God, how can you talk that way?"

She ran to hide and Fräulein Irma's laughter followed her.

Across the way was the Czechoslovakian concentration camp, where some tens of thousands of Czechoslovakian Jewish fami-lies were kept. They did not go through the "bath" and families were not separated. They were led into the camp straight from the train together with all their baggage. Everyone envied them.

Some of them would occasionally throw across a piece of bread for Dvora Leah and the children.

Today, Rosh Hashana eve, they all had to give back their clothes and shoes—to be disinfected, so they were told. But at night, trucks came by, packed the families into them and shipped them off to the crematories.

This first night of Rosh Hashana trembled with their soul-rending weeping.

The frightening cries awoke all the surrounding camps.

The next morning no one could swallow their drops of soup and pieces of bread. They got cramps and felt as if their intestines had been wrung.

It was the same with Dvora Leah. Rivkale, too, doubled up with pain. Fräulein Irma's laughter came back to her and she thought again about the weird explanation of the burning in the ovens and the inscription on the belt-buckle—"God with us."

It was a lovely day. The sky was pure blue and the grass was turning yellow. From the few young trees, withered leaves were falling; a light breeze tossed them about. White networks of webs swayed between the branches. Insects buzzed. The air was filled with the smell of burnt human flesh. Every once in a while, a light breeze swept by, bringing in its sway clouds of fresh air. It was a typical golden Polish autumn day. The concentration-camp prisoners warmed themselves in the sun. Some sat beside the walls of the barracks; some stretched out on the lime paths; others stood in little groups talking politics, commenting on the news which reached them from the underground radio. Rivkale sat on the ground and watched the distant mountains which were encircled by black clouds. People told her that these were the Carpathian Mountains, and that the clouds were forests.

Rivkale thought how lucky she would be if she could be there now. She would be as free as a bird. Rivkale played with the sand, poured it on one bare foot, packed it down with her little hands, pulled her foot out and an oven was formed. She hummed a ghetto song:

> Our Jewish police
> Bid us hold the peace,

You'll know of no need
There will be plenty to feed.

Her mind turned to the future: it's after the war and she is together with mommy and daddy. They live in the same house as before. She has a whole bed to herself. She goes to school, studies well and her teacher likes her. She comes home, kisses her mommy and daddy and her brother Simkhale. On the table lies a *whole* loaf of bread; she helps herself to as much as she wants. She eats so much! Nearly the entire bread. Then she is served a plateful of potatoes. She offers some bread and potatoes to her cousin Sarahle. They eat until they're full. Both are in the same class and they are going home to do their homework. Rivkale lifted her eyes from the sand and saw Fräulein Irma coming. She jumped up and ran away breathlessly, but the hunting dog caught up with her and dragged her to the ground. It wouldn't move from the spot until Irma Greiser came up.

When Fräulein Irma Greiser paraded over the camp, no prisoner was allowed to be on the road. Everyone had either to run into the ditches or behind the walls of the barracks. They had to know that here was a member of the "master race."

This time, too, everyone dispersed like doves sighting an eagle. Only one woman remained on the road. Irma Greiser strutted over to her.

"You swine! Don't you know that when I walk by you must jump into the ditch!"

"I came just yesterday so I didn't know," the woman answered. She wore eyeglasses, so Irma Greiser told her to take them off. Then she took them away from her, smiling politely. The woman became composed. Soon, however, her face was covered with cuts from the leather whip which Irma Greiser was never without.

The woman tried to protect her eyes with her hands and these two became badly cut and were bleeding. She wept frightfully and fell to the ground. Irma Greiser kicked and beat her.

"Stand up!" she ordered.

The woman pulled herself up with her last bit of strength. "Now you'll know, you swine! I'll educate you yet! This is an educational institute!"

Smiling again, she returned the eyeglasses to the woman. (This was all premeditated since a pair of eyeglasses could be useful for a German and she did not want them broken).

Then, as if nothing had happened, she went over to Rivkale who was being guarded by the hunting dog.

"Why do you run away from me?" she asked her. "I give you food to eat and yet you run away from me!"

She proceeded to instruct Rivkale that she must bow deeply before her and say: "Good morning!" At the same time Fräulein Irma swung her knotted leather whip in the air, as if saying: "Do you see? Your life is in my hands!"

Rivkale was overcome by fear and continued to lie with her face against the ground. "Stand up!" Irma Greiser sharply ordered her. Rivkale rose quickly and stood at attention. Fräulein Greiser enjoyed this tremendously.

"Oh, so you're letting yourself be educated!"

She then took out a piece of bread with horsemeat sausage and stretched it out to Rivkale. Rivkale tried to reach for it, but Irma Greiser pulled her hand back. When Rivkale was put through this several times, Irma Greiser threw the food to the dog. The dog jumped up and caught it. You could hear his teeth clamp shut.

Rivkale cringed and broke into mournful tears. Holding her sides, Irma Greiser broke into uncontrollable laughter. She took out another piece of bread and gave it to Rivkale.

"Ha-ha-ha! You donkey! You dirty little thing. You were afraid there wouldn't be any for you."

Rivkale swallowed the bread like a hungry wolf. Tears ran down her hollow cheeks.

"You eat like a wild beast. What sort of animals are the Jews! My dog eats more politely! Look at him! . . . Learn how to eat!"

She laughed and threw the dog another portion.

When Rivkale finished the piece of bread, Irma took her by the hand and they walked off together.

The prisoners dispersed in a hurry.

For the smallest "transgression" she used to penalize the prisoners by making them stand barefoot on hot coals, the dog watching that the victims didn't move about or scream. If they did—he taught them discipline with his wolflike teeth as Irma Greiser yelled:

"This is an educational institute! I will educate these dirty Jews!"

Irma and Rivkale walked over a small bridge, crossing a canal used as a refuse disposal unit. The canal was especially constructed in such a way that the prisoners had to lie flat on their stomachs to clean it.

Not everyone was fortunate enough to clean the canal. You had to have influence, for such work put you in a special category and entitled you to an extra portion of soup.

Irma Greiser pointed to the deep canal and asked Rivkale sadistically:

"Shall I throw you in?"

She caught Rivkale by the dress and raised her over the side of the bridge. Rivkale clasped Irma's hand and gasped for breath.

"I'll throw you down there! You'll swim in your father's ashes!" she laughed.

"Don't throw me in!" Rivkale wept and begged.

"Don't cry. I can't stand crying," winced Fräulein Irma.

The prisoners in the distance were afraid to look; they wanted to shrivel up and vanish.

"There, I'm going to throw you down!" she screamed.

"Mommy! Mommy!" Rivkale cried pitifully.

Dvora Leah could not hear, for she was in another part of the camp. Irma Greiser laughed sadistically. Rivkale felt as if her heart would stop beating as her breath ran short.

Suddenly Irma Greiser lifted Rivkale as high as her hands would reach and set her down on the bridge.

"You donkey; you can't take a joke! Away you dirty little devil! Ha-ha-ha!"

Rivkale, weeping, ran to her mother, followed by Irma Greiser's laughter.

Even though Dvora Leah was the wife of an engineer she still kept the traditional religious beliefs in which she was brought up.

Her parents were not happy that their daughter married an engineer and that the marriage was a love match. Later they felt better about it when they saw that their daughter kept a strictly *kosher* home.

Her husband gave in to her in all things. Dvora Leah didn't even allow her name to be changed. Her husband wanted to call her Lola, but she insisted on being called by her true name, the name given her at birth.

One thing in particular she observed strictly—the lighting of the Sabbath candles. It wasn't the easiest thing to carry out in the concentration camp, but overcoming all difficulties she managed to secure candles. Everyone wondered how she got candles each week, but this was her own secret. In Auschwitz it was impossible to obtain candles, so Dvora Leah risked her life, stole over to the kitchen, and looked through the potato peels in the hope of finding some small potatoes. The camp head, Irma Greiser, once caught her in the act and forced her to walk barefoot on hot coals.

Dvora Leah took her punishment with love and thanked the Almighty that she was spared a searching. She had four potatoes hidden in her bosom. Dvora Leah prayed: "Only for you, beloved God, do I do it so that I might keep the holy commandment. By the mercy of my parents, by the merit of my husband (he was already gassed, but she did not know it) and that of my little children who are too young to sin, I pray that I may escape from her clutches!"

Dvora Leah took her piece of wood and bored little holes in each of the four potatoes. She pulled some threads from her dress and made them into wicks. She always put aside half of her ration of margarine and now filled these holes with it and dipped the wicks in the margarine. And so at last she had little candles to light.

She also carved and peeled the potatoes and in time when they dried out and were soaked through in fat, they took on the appearance of real candles. You couldn't recognize that these were once potatoes.

Dvora Leah vowed that she would keep these candle-holders as her holiest tokens of remembrance. After the war she would decorate her Sabbath and holiday table with these very candle-holders.

Once, Dvora Leah together with four other women of the barracks, bought the *Megillos* (Ecclesiastes, Ruth, Esther, Lamentations, and Song of Songs) in I.L. Peretz's Yiddish translation, which had been smuggled in at the station. Each of the women gave a quarter portion of bread for this book. Dvora Leah taught Rivkale how to read from this sacred work.

A group of women also used to gather in a corner of the barracks and listen to Dvora Leah read chapters from *The Song of Songs*, from *The City of Slaughter* (I.L. Peretz had translated into Yiddish this work of Chaim Nachman Bialik) and from the *Book of Lamentations*. On hearing *The Song of Songs* they were carried away into a distant world of love and nature, forgetting where they were.

In the *Book of Lamentations* they saw their own ruination as if the prophet were describing it. The present catastrophe was not a novel occurrence. Jews survived nevertheless as a nation. They would survive again. They saw the same vision in

The City of Slaughter. At the lines: "Where is the fist? Where is the thunder that will settle the reckoning for all the generations?" their hands turned into fists and their hearts burned for revenge.

When Dvora Leah put away this sacred book, she kissed it just as she would a prayer book. After lighting the Sabbath candles she had a feeling of elation and her heart was lighter. Sometimes, after the blessing of the candles, she would say: "Children, we shall be saved; it seems to me we are saved already!"

The barracks chief, twenty-two-year-old Fräulein Pollack, was here with her mother who was camp *Kapo* (head of the *Kapos*). Fräulein Pollack came from a village in Slovakia. When she came to the city she was sixteen years old. A pimp befriended her and turned her into a prostitute, and her mother became a keeper of a brothel. Both were illiterate, but here in Auschwitz they came to power. They were among the prominent people of the camp. Fräulein Pollack often awoke from her sleep, screaming: "Don't shoot me!"

The story was this: Fräulein Pollack had been in Auschwitz only several weeks when the SS chose her and four other women to be shot. They drove the naked women with the help of dogs against the firing-line wall, tied the women's hands and blindfolded them. They shot them one by one. Fräulein Pollack was the last to be shot, but instead of aiming at her the SS shot into the wall. They did this at least ten times. The officer in charge untied her hands and removed the blindfold. She no longer knew where in the world she was. He asked her whether she wanted to live, but she could neither hear what he said nor could she answer. It took some time before she realized what was happening.

"Do you want to live?" he repeated.

"*Jawohl*," she cried out hysterically and fell to his feet weeping. "Don't shoot me!" she screamed.

"Well, good! From now on you will be well off. You will have plenty to eat. You'll be barracks chief. If you don't keep order and enforce the rules, I will hang you myself. Understand?"

"*Jawohl!*"

Since then, Fräulein Pollack knew only one thing: the harder she drove her prisoners, the better life would be for her. Everyone trembled before her. She settled her accounts here; took revenge on the finer women whom she always regarded enviously. She had plenty to eat and drink and looked robust. She wore nice clothes which were given to her by a "Canadian" with whom she was carrying on a romance. She gloried in parading before the naked women wearing her new clothes. Her heart swelled with joy as the taste of revenge comforted her. More than one prisoner recognized her own dress or the dress of one of her relatives on her.

Fräulein Pollack handed out severe penalties to gain favor in the eyes of the SS. She was constantly afraid of making a slip and ending her illustrious career.

One day, when the women were outside for the roll call, Fräulein Pollack carried out a search of her own (she did this quite often) and found the *Megillos*. She had no way of knowing to whom the book belonged, but the image of herself against the firing wall rose before her eyes. She ran out on the square and shouted furiously:

"Whose *Siddur* is this?" When no one came to claim it, she shouted even more terrifyingly:

"Tell me whose *Siddur* this is, or else I'll punish you all! For the last time—speak!"

When she realized that no one was going to tell her, she swung her club at the row of women and ordered them to jump about like frogs:

"You want to ruin me?" she screamed as she saw herself again at the firing wall. "You still believe in God? They burn you here alive—rabbis too! If there were a God he wouldn't allow this! Stupid! Whose *Siddur* is this? Tell me!

"No one's talking? In that case keep this *exercise* going for two hours!" she screamed.

As the women were jumping about like frogs, the camp head, Fräulein Irma Greiser, arrived. The firing wall in all its clarity shot up before her eyes.

In the concentration camp, the Jews had to salute the Germans, but were never saluted in return. Irma Greiser was very pleased with her barracks head, Fräulein Pollack, and she returned her salute with a smile. Fräulein Pollack told her the story and showed her the book.

Irma Greiser became enraged. Whenever she saw Jewish writing she burned up with fury.

"A Bible!" she screamed. "Where did you find this shit—you stinkpots, gang of criminals! To whom does it belong? You had better tell me or else I'll hang every tenth slut!"

She waited several seconds but no one came out.

"For the last time: To whom does this dirty Bible belong!

"Tell me voluntarily or else I'll hang every tenth stinking figure!

"You have three minutes!"

Irma Greiser held the watch in her hand and waited.

The last few months of her father's life passed before Dvora Leah's mind. For 46 years, her father, Reb Aaron, was cantor and *shokhet* in the town of Sonick.

He was known to the whole surrounding territory as a wise and honest person. Jews and non-Jews came to him for advice. His door was always open for the needy.

The Jews gave Reb Aaron the title of "the father," for he was, indeed, a father to orphans and widows.

Impoverished brides always received financial aid through him. He married off many orphans, providing the dowry himself.

In the year nineteen hundred and thirty-nine, when the Germans invaded Poland, Reb Aaron went to even greater trouble to help people. Transients were never left without a home. He helped them escape, blessing them as they left on their perilous journeys.

He opened a kitchen for the refugees who passed through the town. He did not part with his beard or sideburns, as did the others, in order to save himself. Reb Aaron had a noble countenance. He was tall, handsome, and stood straight as an oak tree. But several days after the Germans arrived, his hair turned gray and his shoulders stooped.

When the Gestapo walked into the Jewish Council and saw Reb Aaron, one of them put the question to him:

"You Jew, are you the elder?"

Reb Aaron thought he meant this in terms of years, so he answered:

"Yes."

The eighteen-year-old Gestapo punk then ordered:

"*Jawohl*! You are now the elder of the Jews! You are answerable for everyone! You must carry out everything the Germans enforce here. If you, Jew, sabotage, you'll get it! This is the Gestapo speaking! Understand, Jew?"

When Reb Aaron heard the word "Gestapo" he felt his legs growing weak.

On his way out, the Gestapo officer ordered that next Sunday the *Judenrat* must supply: ten beds complete with bedding, ten roast ducks, five cases of whiskey, five barrels of beer and ten pretty young women.

From that time on the Gestapo notices and orders were posted in the town under Reb Aaron's name.

Reb Aaron wanted to resign. He didn't want to be a plaything in the hands of the Germans. He was not allowed to resign, for there was no one to take his place. He finally thought perhaps it was the will of God that it be so, that he again represent the Jewish community as he did in the past 46 years, ever since Jews settled in this town.

But Reb Aaron did not carry out a single order the way the Germans wanted.

He did everything he could to avoid harming his brethren.

On the Fast of Esther, in the year nineteen hundred and forty-one, the Gestapo ordered Reb Aaron to provide ten Jews who were to be hanged the next day and to have a gallows constructed in the square by 5 o'clock.

Reb Aaron knew they meant it and so answered that three he could provide—those directly in his charge. The first victim was himself; the second, his wife; the third, his youngest unmarried daughter. (The Germans had shot her fiancé immediately upon marching into Poland, on Yom Kippur, together with many other worshippers whom they drove out of the synagogue still wrapped in their prayer shawls.)

The Gestapo secured the remaining seven Jews themselves. One of the victims was the owner of the flour mill in Sonick. A native German, who had connections with the Gestapo, had been given the job of managing the mill. The Jew remained on as a worker, but now this manager saw the opportunity to rid himself of the former owner. Three other Jews were caught while leaving the ghetto to get a few potatoes to still the hunger of their children. The remaining three were from another town, but had joined the ghetto of Sonick.

During the entire night in prison, Reb Aaron read the Psalms. All were in one cell. When one of the men cried out: "How can I leave my wife and children?" Reb Aaron consoled him and then took him to task for weeping. "Not everyone merits this!" he exclaimed. "We are going to save a city of Jews. We are to sanctify the name of God. That is the most precious of deeds! Remember," he appealed to all of them, "tomorrow you must go to the gallows with uplifted heads! *Kiddush Hashem*—to die sanctifying God's Name—is a great honor!"

The gallows which stood in the middle of the market square had a frightening effect. No one in the ghetto slept that night.

Each felt the departure of Reb Aaron as a personal loss that could never be reclaimed.

*   *   *

Next day, in the morning, at a quarter after ten, the whole ghetto population gathered in the marketplace. They were surrounded by military police who were armed with machine guns. This was the "party" which the Germans prepared for the Jewish feast of Purim.

(Hitler had said a few days earlier: "The Jews will not be joyous this Purim!" The Jews read it in the smuggled German newspapers.)

In the middle of the marketplace stood a newly erected gallows. The Gestapo arrived in a car and the "disciplinary service" (Jewish police) brought in the ten Jews. The first to arrive was Reb Aaron, dressed in his *kittel* (white robe) with a prayer shawl covering him. He was no longer stooped but walked erect with firm steps.

They all thought they would find Reb Aaron a broken man, full of sorrow. Instead, he walked with a steady step, ecstatic, as he used to look on his way to rescue Jews.

When the ten stood under the gallows, the Gestapo officer read out their sentence:

"Ten Jews, war criminals, are sentenced to death. *Heil Hitler!*"

The noose was thrown over Reb Aaron's neck first. They heard him murmur a blessing with the same emotion and tone with which he led the prayers in the synagogue, rending the heavens and sending the prayers of the congregation to the Holy Throne.

When the noose was on all of them and the Gestapo officer made a sign to drop the hatch, they all cried out:

"Hear, O Israel!"

Whoever looked at Reb Aaron was reminded of his, "Hear O Israel, the Lord is our God, the Lord is one," that he chanted while removing the Torah from the Holy Ark.

These thoughts were passing through Dvora Leah's mind and finally she said to herself: "Just like my father, of blessed memory, I too must be ready for *Kiddush Hashem*—to die for the sanctification of God's Name."

She stepped out of the line and declared boldly:

"The Bible is mine!"

Fräulein Greiser was taken aback and looked at her in astonishment.

Dvora Leah was holding Simkhale in her arms. Rivkale stood near her, holding onto her mother.

She stood barefooted, dressed in rags. Her head was shaven and her face was hollow and sunken. Only the eyes were aglow, proclaiming her as a human being; black Jewish eyes, reflecting the suffering of millions.

These eyes, bold and fearless, turned toward Irma Greiser, who stood tall and slim in her SS uniform of the best woolen materials, in shining officer boots, one hand holding the knotted leather whip and the other thrust in her leather belt where she carried her revolver and cartridges.

Both women stood for some seconds without speaking, looking straight into each other's eyes, sizing one another up, testing each other.

Then for a moment Dvora Leah triumphed over Irma Greiser, the ruler of Auschwitz, who experienced her own insignificance in the sight of Dvora Leah. Soon, however, she regained her control.

"Do you want to hang?" she snapped. She paused for a few seconds and then said again, quietly:

"No, the Bible doesn't belong to you! You're not responsible!"

"I am responsible," Dvora Leah insisted.

"Where was the Bible hidden?"

Dvora Leah described the spot and the barracks chief, Fräulein Pollack, confirmed it.

A deathly silence descended upon the crowd of women.

"You think this is a sanatorium," Irma Greiser began sternly. "You do nothing, just eat and shit! This is an educational institute! Dirty criminal race! Why don't you let yourself be educated! You deserve to be hanged for this criminal act! But since she confessed voluntarily and is the mother of two children— she'll get fifty on the ass!"

With lightning speed two *Kapos* brought the strapping bench to the square.

They took the children away from the mother and stretched her across the bench. Her hands and feet rested on the ground board where they were secured in presses. The two *Kapos*, using their rubber clubs and with the rhythm of two smiths forging hot iron, counted out fifty blows. Dvora Leah was forced to follow rhythmically: "One! Two! Three! . . ."

At the 22nd she became silent. The children wept mournfully.

In the meantime, in the far end of the camp, flames of fire, like from smelting works, poured out from the four red-brick crematories. The air was filled with the stench of smoldering bones.

When they took the bench away, Irma Greiser ordered a fire to be made. With the zeal of someone engaged in a holy task, she placed the book into the flames.

When the fire had burnt itself out, she ordered them back into the barracks.

When the women revived Dvora Leah and put cold water to her open wounds, she said to them:

"Now I am like my pious father," and she added, "my father, may he rest in peace, used to quote his rabbi: 'Fools! They think they can burn these words which are more precious than gold. Those are words of flaming fire—how can fire consume them?'"

Next day Dvora Leah told her friends of the following dream she had: "On a huge square, thousands of Germans assembled— civilians and soldiers. On the road stretched a column of exiled, exhausted Jews, their infants in their arms, dragging their packs and valises after them. They were being driven by the SS, who were riding on motorcycles. Suddenly the Germans fell upon the Jews, took away everything, even tore the clothes off their backs, beating them, piercing them with bayonets. The road became filled with corpses and the air with crying and weeping. The blood flowed on the road and the Germans licked it up. In a moment the scene changed. There was a dark cell. Inside, sprawled in blood, lay two frightfully hateful-looking animals— their ears were cut off, their eyes pierced, their tails chopped off and their hides skinned. It was nauseating to look at them. They were a mixture of a hippopotamus, a gorilla, and a chimpanzee. When I looked more closely at them I realized that they were chimpanzees. With their forepaws they played with the blood. They began to fight, biting each other, sucking each other's blood. They panted from overeating.

"Suddenly a man sprang up near them and struck them with his fists. Still the animals would not unclamp their teeth from each other's flesh. The man continued to level his blows on their heads, but the animals were just as adamant. I was at the door. I was overcome with fear. I wanted to run away, and I turned around and saw a hill, drenched with sun, grow before my eyes. Many Jews from my own town were on it. They were dressed in their holiday clothes. It was *Shavuos* and they were eating baked dairy foods. It seemed as if I were in the Land of Israel. I ran towards the hill, breathing heavily. I was quite close already when I dropped to the ground and awoke with alarm."

Dvora Leah paused awhile and then continued:

"I'll interpret the dream myself," she declared. "The war will end soon and the Germans will appear to the world just like these animals in my dream. They will suck the blood from each other, putting an end to themselves. My fall, just short of the peak of the hill, means that, I'm afraid, I will not survive the war," she said mournfully as she looked at her children. "But the Jews will get to *Eretz Israel*, their spirit will be revived, and they will lead a good life!" she concluded.

* * *

Whenever Fräulein Pollack saw Dvora Leah light the Sabbath candles she would beat her murderously. Dvora Leah decided to light the candles very early, so that it would not occur to the barracks chief to spy on her.

Nevertheless, the barracks chiefs had their own informers who told them everything. These informers were repaid with soup, a piece of bread, and were excluded from the "selections."

They did their work well and the prisoners never could discover who they were.

It was past midday. The barracks chief, having stuffed herself full of food, lay down in her room.

Dvora Leah placed three-year-old Simkhale in a corner of the barracks and went to light the Sabbath candles. At that moment, a woman who had been spying on Dvora Leah all day, left and told the barracks chief. The firing-wall rose again before her eyes.

On lighting the first candle, tears fell from Dvora Leah's eyes as she sighed: "For my husband—let him live and be well!"

On lighting the second candle, she sighed again: "For Rivkale—let her live and be well!"

And when she lit the third candle: "For my Simkhale—let him live and be well!"

When she lit the fourth candle, the tears rolled down her sunken cheeks: "For myself and all Jews who cannot light candles and have no one to do it for them!"

She embraced the candle flames and made the blessing: "Blessed art thou, our God, King of the Universe, who sanctified us with His commandments and commanded us to light the Sabbath candles."

Behind her rose the figure of the barracks chief, Fräulein Pollack. She began to beat Dvora Leah.

Dvora Leah bent down to avoid the blows and Fräulein Pollack's club landed on her own knee. She gasped with pain and instinctively threw the club away as if it were at fault. In a moment, however, she came to, grabbed Dvora Leah by the head and threw her to the ground. She jumped on top of her and stamped her with her officer's boots.

"Shoot me! Shoot me!" Dvora Leah implored.

The barracks chief continued to beat her.

Blood spurted from Dvora Leah's head, nose and mouth. Her face and lips were cut and two teeth were knocked out. Fräulein Pollack finally set Dvora Leah on her knees, put two heavy bricks in her hands and ordered her to stretch them out in front of her.

"Stay this way for two hours!" she shouted and instructed the house attendant to watch Dvora Leah.

Disheveled and soaked through with sweat, she went back to her room.

"Oh, God!" Dvora Leah wept.

"How can you allow your children who obey your commandments to be tortured so? Show us that you are a God of Justice! Oh, Father in Heaven, are you or are you not!"

As she wept, Rivkale ran into the barracks, crying sorrowfully after having been tortured by Irma Greiser. She ran to her mother to be consoled.

Dvora Leah knew something frightful had happened to her child.

She threw away the bricks and embraced her daughter. The house attendant stood watching.

Rivkale sobbed frightfully. "Mommy," she gasped. She had not the strength to say more. Mother and child held each other and wept together. Their weeping turned into sobbing, which became quieter and quieter, until only their hearts cried out to each other.

Meanwhile Simkhale awoke from his sleep and began to cry too. A girl brought him to his mother.

The whole barracks of prisoners now gathered to the spot.

The weeping attracted the attention of a Polish political prisoner who worked as a bricklayer. (The men's concentration camp was a great distance away from the women's camp and they never met).

The barracks chief, dressed in her silk pajamas, came strutting in. She formed a path by swinging her club over the heads of the gathered crowd.

"You impudent slut!" she screamed at Dvora Leah. "You and your dirty little brats don't let me sleep!"

She raised her stick at Dvora Leah, but the Pole grabbed her around the throat.

"You pig!" he shouted. "You're going to beat? Torture?" He pressed down so hard on her throat that her tongue almost popped out of her mouth. "I'll pull your head off!"

The political prisoner first broke the stick to pieces and tossed it outside together with the two bricks Dvora Leah was holding.

"If you ever dare beat the prisoners again, I'll turn your whorish body to ashes!" he shouted pointing to the crematory.

The barracks chief became pale and speechless.

"Do you hear?" he turned to the prisoners. "Remember: if she ever lifts her claws again, let me know about it immediately! Even if it costs me my life, this bitch won't get out of my hands alive!"

Fräulein Pollack's spirit was broken, and the women felt avenged.

Next day, in the morning, Dvora Leah went to the infirmary to get some medicine for the wounds inflicted on her by Fräulein Pollack.

Near the infirmary stood the barracks that was occupied by pregnant women and those with infants. This was merely a piece of deception to make the prisoners think the Germans cared for pregnant women and infants.

Every few weeks the Germans cleaned the barracks of all people, saying that the patients were being removed to a recuperation camp. In reality they were sent directly to the crematories. Other patients from new transports were brought in. The pregnant women who were in their late months of pregnancy had to sleep on the upper third bunk.

When Dr. Mengele came in, the barracks chief shouted loudly: "*Achtung!*"

All the women had to jump off their bunks and line up in military formation.

Dr. Mengele shouted, "One, two, three!"

On the count of three, they all had to run back to their bunks. The women who could not manage this any more were sent to the gas chamber. When Dvora Leah passed by this barracks she was overwhelmed with fear.

Dvora Leah had to stand in line at the infirmary. She noticed how the barracks was divided into little rooms, representing different departments: those for internal diseases, the dentistry clinic, the operation room, the delivery room, the reception room and the pharmacy.

All these departments were housed in this one barracks.

This infirmary was created by the Jewish doctors: the Germans did not assist in any way.

The doctors carried out operations with ordinary kitchen knives, sterilizing their tools in soup plates. Medicine kits were smuggled in at the station by the Jewish doctors and pharmacists who brought these things with them. Some doctors used all the skill they possessed to help the sick, but they had little to work with.

The doctors risked their lives. They carried out abortions and in this way tried to save many women from being sent to the crematories. As soon as the midwife took a child, she had to drown it in a pot of cold water in the presence of the camp chief, Fräulein Irma Greiser.

But from time to time, the SS ordered a live infant to be delivered to them.

Irma Greiser would wrap the infant in paper, tie it up with a silk band and play with it. She would take the infant out, smile at it, put it on the ground by the camp gate and have her wolf-like dog sniffle at it. The child cried bitterly. An SS man would finally take the infant away.

The Germans used these infants for their various experiments.

Every expectant mother knew she was a candidate for the ovens. In order to save herself she would sign herself out immediately on the third day and go to work. She dragged herself around with a shovel, digging foxholes. Blood dripped from her, but she watched herself so that the SS would not notice it. Friends helped as much as they were able: they supported her and, when the SS weren't looking, carried her. They themselves produced her quota of work. Nevertheless it was all in vain. She was sent to the crematory in any case. Dvora Leah waited here in vain for several hours. Her wounds burned fiercely, but no doctor appeared. A *Kapo* came running and dispersed the whole line of sick people.

Fräulein Pollack, during a roll call of 28,000 women, picked out one girl, Hinda, to be her servant: to clean her rooms, cook for her, wash and mend.

When the barracks chief took Hinda from the line and told her to come to her room after the count, Hinda's teeth chattered with fright. She knew barracks chief Pollack was the "Beast" the prisoners called her.

Hinda could not understand why the "Beast" asked her to come to her rooms. "It's not a good sign," she thought; "now I must take leave of the world!" She reckoned up her life: she was only six years old when her mother died in childbirth. Her father, a pauper, was left with eight children—one smaller than the next. Strangers took pity on them and wanted to adopt the orphans, but the family would not allow it.

Hinda was taken in by an aunt living in a nearby town. She was ill-treated by her and almost died of starvation. She hadn't a dress to wear, nor a pair of shoes. It pained her to watch her aunt dress her own children so well and serve them better food. Later the children were sent to school and Hinda had to wait on them and take care of the house. She went to bed late and had to rise early. She slept in the kitchen on a bench near the drains.

Each night her tears drenched the single sheet she was given to cover herself with. Another aunt, from a larger city, took pity on her and worked out a plan for her escape. Even to this day Hinda could not forget the fear she experienced during those terrifying hours. It seemed to her that her wicked aunt and uncle were running after her and were already quite near. She breathed more freely once the train began to move.

The second aunt dressed Hinda: bought her several pairs of underclothes, several dresses and two pairs of shoes. She sent her to school and in her spare time Hinda helped keep house and took care of the three children.

The uncle was a very religious man. He spied on Hinda: watched where she went, what she read. She didn't have a single private moment to herself. Secretly she took out books from the Yiddish library and read them at night by the light of a candle. Once the uncle caught Hinda at this. He shouted that books would lead Hinda to apostasy. Hinda had to promise him that she would read no more books. The uncle wanted to marry her to a Yeshiva student, but Hinda resisted. She was in love with the librarian, who was also a tailor's apprentice. They were about to be married when the war broke out. He joined the underground and fell in battle against the Nazis. Then followed her life in the ghetto with its hunger, slave labor, sickness and—Auschwitz.

She came to Auschwitz with her whole family: sisters, brothers, uncles, aunts, father and stepmother. At the station a "Canadian" asked her: "Whose child is that you're carrying?" "My sister's," she answered.

When he wanted to tear the child away from her, her sister ran up and took the child away. "Give me the child. I'll hide it somewhere," the "Canadian" begged her. "No." the sister declared. "If they'll shoot the child, let them shoot me too!" They did not allow Hinda to go along with her uncle and their children; nor with her sisters and their children. She still remembers how her brother-in-law shouted to her sister:

"Toby, I thank you for being so good to me! Take good care of our children!"

Hinda came to Auschwitz from Rumania. In her hometown, the Jewish families remained together until the last moment. When the Russians were approaching, the Germans made a ghetto, gathered all the Jews together and sent them away to Auschwitz.

When Hinda worked outside the ghetto, she saw trains packed, with Jews passing through daily. Through the grated windows, the Jews shouted and begged:

"Take pity on us. Give us some water!"

"Give us candles to light!" women cried.

"Something for the little ones!"

Hinda asked them where they were going.

"We don't know," they answered, "we have been riding like this for six days already!"

Hinda tried to help them with a bit of water, but the guard drove her away, beating her.

The Germans gave the Jews of the ghetto where Hinda was staying three days to pack whatever they wanted to take with them. They were all being sent to work, they were told. They were instructed to take along needles, thread and work tools. Hinda took with her her entire wardrobe and an expensive, beautiful handbag—a gift from her fiancé. In it she kept her documents and photographs of herself, family and friends. She considered this handbag her most prized possession. The journey took four days. It stopped in Warsaw for several hours where the guard was changed. The SS man, a Hungarian, who guarded the car, opened the door slightly and picked out some valuable things for himself. "So long as you are in my hands you have nothing to fear," he said, "but after that, it will be the end of you!" He took Hinda's handbag, examined it. "The Jews have nice things. You won't need this anymore. I'll take it for my fiancée."

At that time (spring of 1944), almost all the transports went directly to the ovens. All four crematoria ovens burned day and night with the Hungarian and Rumanian Jews. Hinda's transport was fortunate in that a "selection" was carried out.

Hinda was an excellent housekeeper. The barracks chief knew it too and chose her from among all the rest.

Immediately after the roll call, the house attendant led Hinda to Fräulein Pollack's rooms.

"What's your name?" were her first words.

"Hinda," she answered, still confused.

"Listen, Hinda, you are very fortunate! You have more luck than brains! Out of the 28,000 prisoners I chose you. You'll want for nothing here; you won't have to stand outside for the count and you'll be free of 'selections.' You'll be my maid and keep my house spotless, wash, mend, bake and cook.

"But you mustn't touch any of the food. If you don't obey all my orders, I'll have you pay for it with your life. You haven't suffered yet; you're from Rumania and gorged and guzzled to the last minute.

"Your life won't be worth a thing if anyone, aside from the two of us, finds out you're cooking extra rations for me.

"Whatever you hear and see—you are to keep quiet about! Do you understand?"

She looked Hinda in the eyes and Hinda answered, still barely composed:

"Yes, I understand."

The barracks chief handed Hinda silk linen, a wool dress, a pair of silk stockings, a silk kerchief and a pair of pretty shoes.

"You mustn't keep a lover!" she said as she handed her the things. "Do you hear?"

She gave Hinda a piece of soap, a comb, a toothbrush and some toothpaste, and told her to wash herself thoroughly.

Hinda did as she was told and Fräulein Pollack herself tied her hair with the silk kerchief.

"Do you see? This is a miracle. You have a small pimple on your face and in the next 'selection' you certainly would have been sent to the ovens. Now you are safe!" she said and slapped her on the back.

The barracks chief's rooms were in the corridor of the barracks, just off the entrance. Across the hall was the food magazine.

Here was stored the food which the barracks chief, with the help of six prisoners, brought from the general storage warehouse each morning. In the barracks chief's room stood a double-bunk with straw bedding covered over with several sheets and pillows. On the lower bunk slept Fräulein Pollack's mother—the camp *Kapo*. On the top bunk slept the barracks chief.

This room also contained a table made of raw boards, four chairs and a chest where the barracks chief kept her best linen, clothes and several pairs of summer and winter shoes.

On the floor lay several rugs.

Underneath the bunk were two boxes containing foodstuffs for cooking and baking; also marmalade, honey, cheese, sausage and margarine. These were the "extras" which the barracks chief stole from the prisoners.

Sometimes she also had the best of wines, pastries, and bottles of chicken fat.

This her lover, the "Canadian," smuggled in for her from the station. They were taken from the Jews who brought these things with them on the transports coming from eastern Europe. They had no idea where they were going, so they brought everything with them.

When the barracks chief left, Hinda washed the floor, dresser, table, chairs, door and windows, and dusted the rugs. She found a piece of red brick, ground it, mixed it with water and a little flour and smeared the stove with it. Then she took some whitewash (from the bricklayer who worked in the camp), mixed it with flour and, using a toothbrush, recoated the lime between the bricks. The tin top and doors she smeared with a bit of rust and water.

When the barracks chief came home she didn't recognize her home; it was so shiny and spotless.

She called in all her friends: the barracks chiefs, house attendants and *Kapos*, and displayed her new home to them.

While Hinda cooked, the barracks chief's mother, the camp *Kapo*, sat outside watching to see that no Germans were coming. The barracks chief herself made as if she were taking a walk on the path. When she saw a German, she signaled to her mother and the old woman would run to Hinda. Hinda would snatch up the foodstuffs and hide them under her own bunk, so that in case of a search the guilt would not fall on Fräulein Pollack.

Hinda roasted food on the dying embers only, to prevent the smell of the food from spreading. On flat plates she baked honey-cakes, butter-cakes, cheese-buns, and cookies.

The camp *Kapo* was also the overseer in the general kitchen and the workers there bribed her with chunks of raw meat. As a result, Hinda roasted meat almost every day.

The barracks chief worried little about securing wood or coal. She left it to Hinda, but this was one of the most difficult things to do in Auschwitz. Without the knowledge of her employer, Hinda bought these in return for food. Fräulein Pollack and her mother also had milk and eggs. These things were originally meant for those suffering from lung diseases, so that they would think that the Germans were really intent on healing them. The overseers stole these things from the sick and exchanged them with Fräulein Pollack for meat and other foodstuffs.

The barracks chief then exchanged this for linen, whiskey, wine, cigarettes, and matches.

Sometimes a prisoner stole some food from Hinda's bunk. Fräulein Pollck would beat her fiercely. "You are responsible for it!" she screamed.

Fräulein Pollack kept constant watch over Hinda to make sure she wasn't eating any of her things. Hinda moved in constant fright and eventually her health broke down and she became ill. One day she told Fräulein Pollack she would rather stand outside for the roll call and for "selections" than be tortured by her and live in constant fear. What is the use of it all? She doesn't want any more of her "favors" and would rather be like the other prisoners.

Fräulein Pollack knew that she would never find another maid like Hinda and she promised she wouldn't hurt her anymore.

When Hinda discovered that Fräulein Pollack and her mother did not finish their food but discarded a good part of it, she began to help herself to the foods even before she served it. Secretly she also gave some to Dvora Leah and the children. This strengthened Dvora Leah's belief that she would survive the war.

In time, Hinda became bolder in her demands on Fräulein Pollack. In the same camp, but in another barracks, lived her two younger sisters and she got Fräulein Pollack to have them move in with her. Hinda helped her sisters with food. When the barracks chief caught Hinda at this, she became furious: "Why do you do this?" she shouted. Hinda told her that she could not stand by while her sisters starved. "What are your sisters to you?" she screamed. "They won't survive the war anyway! You still have some hope!"

"If my sisters won't survive the war, I don't want to either!" Hinda answered, weeping.

From now on, Dvora Leah and the children received a little soup from Hinda every day. Hinda took the soup from the noon distribution when the house attendant brought Fräulein Pollack half a pot of soup. They never distributed a just measure of soup to the prisoners and with what they stole in this way they bought themselves portions of bread, clothes, and cigarettes. Hinda couldn't bear it, and she took the pot of soup and distributed it among the prisoners. The barracks chief beat her, but it didn't make any difference. The following day she did the same thing.

"What shall I do?" she argued, "if I can't stand to see soup being wasted by us and outside people drop from hunger!"

"You're a real *kosher* idiot!" Fräulein Pollack laughed at her.

Whenever a heavy rain fell, Fräulein Pollack would drive the prisoners from the barracks. This was done on the order of the SS, so that at the 'selections' Dr. Mengele would find prisoners who caught cold and coughed and sneezed. The women wore only a thin rag and went barefooted.

Even though Hinda was free of this, she now ran out into the rain and stood together with her sisters.

Fräulein Pollack searched the whole barracks for Hinda, but did not find her. Finally she discovered her among the prisoners, standing in the heavy downpour.

"You don't have to stand here. Go into the barracks. Don't be an idiot!"

"If the others have to stand here and my sisters too, then I'll stand here too!"

The barracks chief fell upon her, swung her stick at her and cried:

"What sort of an idiot are you?"

Under a volley of blows, she drove Hinda back to her rooms.

"If you are going to act like an idiot—I'll have to educate you with the stick! You could be very fortunate if only you had brains!"

She gave Hinda several pairs of socks to mend for her lover, the "Canadian."

The rain kept coming down and the women outside cried and screamed. They begged Fräulein Pollack to have pity on them and let them back in the barracks. Dvora Leah hid Simkhale under her dress at her bosom. Rivkale was protected from the rain by the bodies of other women.

Hinda couldn't sit still. When Fräulein Pollack fell asleep, she stole out. She brought a cover for Dvora Leah and the children, and remained standing with her sisters.

The sisters took her to task for being so stubborn. "We have to stand here! But your presence won't make us feel any better. We are happy that at least one of us doesn't have to suffer."

"When I suffer with you, I feel better," Hinda answered.

The rain poured down incessantly, accompanied by thunder and lightning.

When the barracks chief arose from her afternoon nap and

saw that Hinda was not in, she ran out again and drove Hinda back into the barracks. "If you are such an idiot and insist on breaking the rules you'll go directly to the ovens in the next 'selection!'"

That same night (*Hashana Rabba*), while the prisoners were sleeping, the SS sent in an order to the barracks chief. She passed the word on to the house attendant and *Kapos*. Quickly all the lights in the barracks were turned on.

"Rise! Rise!" the guards screamed. "Everyone line up on one side! Everybody to the right!"

The women, completely naked, were placed on one side of the barracks.

The "bread-gorgers," as Dr. Mengele called them, remained sitting.

Three days ago Dr. Mengele had picked out the healthiest and more robust of the women prisoners and gave each of them a whole loaf of bread and half a sausage. They were guarded to make sure they did not share it with the others. Their joy was boundless, but this aroused an immeasurable envy and hatred in the other women. Next day several "doctors," their stuffed cheeks glowing red, came for these "bread-gorgers." The "doctors" wore butcher aprons and their sleeves were rolled up to display their bulging muscles. They had the appearance of hog-slaughterers and cast a fearful spell on everyone.

They took the women away and drained pints of blood from them. (The Germans used the blood for their wounded soldiers).

The women just managed to crawl back to the barracks. They soon lost their reason and looked like corpses. From that time on they were not able to support themselves on their feet.

Hinda wanted to stand in line with the others, but the barracks chief wouldn't let her.

"You're really an ass, but you have a good heart. You must live through this and be happy. What an ass you are!"

"That's nice of you," Hinda answered, "but if my sisters must stand for "selections" I must too!"

"Wait!" Fräulein Pollack cried out, holding her back. Tears streamed from her eyes.

Hinda could not believe it. Before she could say another word, Fräulein Pollack pulled Hinda's two sisters from the row and sent all three into the barracks.

Meanwhile, Dr. Mengele, a cigarette in his mouth, together with Irma Greiser and two SS men stormed in.

Dr. Mengele fixed his eyes on the women, looking for blemishes and deformities.

He listened for a cough, a sneeze, a gasp or a cry. Everyone in Auschwitz knew his life was in Dr. Mengele's hands. The women were like cattle before slaughter.

He worked quickly:

"Right! Left! Right! Left!" he shouted as he pointed with his forefinger in the two directions.

Seven-year-old Rivkale told her mother she would stand in a corner; perhaps God would work a miracle and Dr. Mengele would not notice her. Rivkale did so, but the German could not be by-passed so easily. He found her out and led her away.

Dr. Mengele was dressed in his SS uniform covered over with medals and ribbons. He always wore his best uniform when he went out on his rounds. He was tall and handsome. The prisoners referred to him as the "Angel of Death in the guise of the Good Angel."

When he came to the "bread-gorgers" he made a quick sign to the left.

When he had completed his "selection" of one-half of the barracks, he turned about and noticed two girls clinging and kissing each other. He went back and asked them calmly why they were kissing. "We are sisters," they said "and are happy that we have remained together."

Dr. Mengele did not speak a word. With a little smile on his face he took one away.

Dvora Leah, carrying her three-year-old Simkhale, stood last in the line. "Perhaps," she thought, "God will work a miracle."

She didn't know that Rivkale was already taken away.

When Dr. Mengele saw them, he walked up and declared: "You stay here. The child goes!"

"If you take the child, I go too!" Dvora Leah answered.

"No. You stay here!" he said sternly.

Dr. Mengele wanted to tear the child from Dvora Leah's arms, but Simkhale bound his arms around his mother's neck and would not let go. It was as hard to tear him from his mother as a branch from a tree. He cried like a sick kitten. Dvora Leah implored Dr. Mengele to be allowed to go with her child.

When Dr. Mengele finally tore the child away, the mother became transformed into a fierce toger and she dug her nails into his eyes.

"Murderer! Give me back my child!" she screamed.

Dr. Mengele drew his revolver and fired several shots. Mother and child fell to the ground, clutching each other.

"Revenge!" she cried out.

Dr. Mengele, his revolver drawn, ran to search every corner of the barracks. Irma Greiser and the SS followed him. They looked and searched the corridor and food magazine. Then they ran into the barracks chief's rooms.

"What are you doing here?" he asked Hinda.

"I'm the maid," she answered. He saw from her outfit that she was telling the truth. He was about to leave when it occurred to him to look under the bunk. He bent down and pulled out Hinda's two sisters. The girls looked like corpses.

"What's this filth doing here?" he shouted at the barracks chief: "You swinish dog. Crucifiers!"

Fräulein Pollack tried to speak, but Dr. Mengele shouted: "Hold your tongue!"

He fired into her several times. Fräulein Pollack fell onto the bunk, groaned frightfully, rolled over, and collapsed on the floor.

Dr. Mengele sent the two girls to the left. Hinda he ordered to remain.

When the "selected" prisoners were led out, Hinda stole in among them and went to the crematory together with her sisters.

Rivkale was placed in a children's barracks. The children were picked as candidates for the crematories. The children knew why they were gathered there. Some of them cried:

"Daddy, Mommy, save us!"

"I still want to live!"

"I don't want to be burned!"

Others looked about, struck dumb.

The barracks was closely guarded by the SS. Small windows opened to the roof. Rivkale suggested that they try to escape through these windows.

The children stood one upon the other and some managed to climb onto the roof.

Rivkale was the pathfinder; she was the first to climb out.

She lay on the roof, hardly breathing, and looked down below where the SS officer, rifle drawn, was patrolling.

It began to rain. She waited a minute until the SS man turned the corner and then let herself down from the roof, followed by several other children.

The darkness was suddenly pierced by lightning. Shots rent the air. Several of the children were hit and dropped to the ground, blood flowing from their wounds. Rivkale managed to escape into the latrine. She crawled through on the toilet seats and hid herself under the floor. She spent the night there.

The next morning (*Shemini Atzeres*) Rivkale heard the prisoners discuss the slaughter of the night before.

"Not a single barracks was spared the killings. The older people went straight to the ovens. That's how it is here: you come through the gate and go out through the chimney. The SS put all the children in one barracks. There is talk they will be burned on *Simkhas Torah*."

Rivkale lay hidden in the latrine a whole day and a whole night without eating. She shivered from cold. It occurred to no one that someone lay hidden there.

On the second day Rivkale heard another discussion among the prisoners.

"There's a child missing. One child escaped that night, so the SS say. They found six of the children dead after the shooting. The SS have announced that if the missing child is not found by four o'clock this afternoon, they'll carry out a 'selection' and for the one child they will take a hundred."

The thought disturbed Rivkale. "One hundred for me! Can I do that? Can I save myself at the expense of one hundred? No . . . I am still young. I want to live! It's nearly the end of the war. I don't want to be burned alive! I'll wait; maybe the SS don't mean it. Everything may turn out all right!"

Every barracks chief counted her prisoners all day long. They chased some away and counted again. They thought the child would eventually show up from her hiding-place and give herself up. But it was in vain. Everywhere the numbers indicated one missing.

The whole camp was now in a turmoil. They knew what a "selection" meant. When they said a hundred, they meant a thousand. Everyone was afraid she would be the one to be taken.

At three o'clock the bell sounded and everyone was ordered into the barracks.

Rivkale heard the confusion. "The slaughter is beginning!" she heard one woman say to another.

In every barracks the women were lined up for "selection." The barracks chiefs counted the women again; the house attendants and *Kapos* searched every corner of the camp.

The SS stood waiting for the arms of the clock to approach four.

Rivkale, still hidden under the floor of the latrine, continued to battle with herself—give herself up or not. Suddenly she remembered how they wanted to hang every tenth woman because of the *Megillos* her mother had hidden. Her mother had confessed voluntarily. "Shall I let a hundred others go to their death on my account? No!" she declared firmly. "I will go the same way as my Mommy!"

Rivkale relived the entire incident. She saw her mother walking out from the line and boldly declaring to Irma Greiser—the queen of Auschwitz—"I am the guilty one! The Bible is mine!"

Every barracks was now ready to proceed with the "selection." The barracks chiefs looked at the clock. There were still ten minutes to four.

In the entire camp one could not hear one single human sound—only the angel of death hovering by. The air was filled with the stench of smoldering bones. The children's barracks was still patrolled by the SS. Their steps resounded through the camp. They looked at their watches: it was still eight minutes before four. They yawned with boredom.

Suddenly, as if rising from the ground, a little girl appeared, her arms raised high. Everyone turned to look. The SS drew their rifles, but the little girl cried out with all her strength:

"Sirs! I'm the girl who ran away! That is me!"

The SS sent word to headquarters that the child had given herself up willingly. Soon the order returned that the "selection" had been canceled.

In the barracks they kissed each other and cried with joy.

When Rivkale came into the barracks the children ran up to her and asked her why she had come back. "At least you would have saved yourself," they told her.

Rivkale told them about her mother. "Little brothers and sisters," she ended, "let us die boldly! Let us all cry out: Hear, O Israel!"

All the children cried out in one voice:

"Hear, O Israel, the Lord is our God, the Lord is One!"

*   *   *

That same evening, when the whole camp stood for the roll call, a "selection" was carried out. Dr. Mengele picked out another six thousand women. Rivkale was sent to the crematory, together with the other children.

All night long the flames spurted from the chimney of the crematories.

Dvora Leah followed in the footsteps of her father, Reb Aaron, and like him died for the sanctification of God's Name.

Rivkale, too, followed in the footsteps of her mother and her grandfather and died for the sanctification of God's Name.

ers running through the streets clutching their little ones and crying frantically, "*Where shall I hide you? Where shall I hide you?*" He heard his elders praying to God to relieve them of their souls and grant them a Jewish burial. He heard the all-pervading lamentation. His frightened but stubborn eyes saw men and women with their loved ones desperately jump from the highest buildings to their death. He felt the terror that they escaped. He saw the Gestapo ripping out doors and floors in their search, combing the garrets and cellars, taking now, indiscriminately, the robust and healthy with the weak and ailing. The Jews did not know where they were being sent but they had a presentiment that it was to their death.

Then on the second day of Rosh Hashana, Berele's own family was taken. They did not go voluntarily as so many had done: the police forced them out. But they had prepared for the inevitable: their pitiful bundles were already packed. There were his father, his mother, his three elder sisters and little Simkhale, his younger brother. Only Berele himself remained hidden, terrified, breathless until they had gone. Then, still fearfully, he crept from hiding to the window, and peered into the courtyard.

He saw the people, his family, the neighbors, men, women, and children lined up in a row by the wall. He saw Gestapo-Officer Schmidt picking out the Jews, pointing with his forefinger, like the venomous tongue of a serpent: "*Right! . . . Left! . . . Right! . . . Left! . . .* " After that he saw him brandishing a white-gloved hand; and a horse-drawn wagon drew up. The people were driven onto it as if they were cattle, as if they were indeed cattle to the slaughter. For some of them the spell of acquiescence was broken and they pleaded piteously. Others attempted to jump off the wagon but they were cruelly beaten back. There were many skirmishes as hysterical mothers crying: "*My only treasures! My life! How can I save you?*" were separated from their children. There were more wagons now. Some of the mothers succeeded in joining their children; those who were still fit for work were kept back.

As the mobilization proceeded, the pandemonium increased and suddenly Berele stiffened. He saw Simkhale jump off the wagon and remain as if glued to the ground. A policeman lashed at him but he refused to move. He was beaten again and again until he was besmeared with blood and thrown back onto the wagon.

There seemed no hope for these condemned Jews. But a mixture of pity and corruption, a loaf of bread for the police or a discreet turning of the head on the part of one or two policemen enabled some to escape—just as rumor had it that even at the final Gathering Point some were able to evade death if gold and diamonds changed hands.

Then Berele heard the voices of other children happily singing. These were the children from the orphanage. They were festively dressed, their hair washed and combed and they were carrying packets of food. In their innocence they thought they were off on a picnic. It was a merry Polish song they were singing:

> The train that comes from far away
> It will not wait a minute.
> So off to Warsaw for a holiday,
> Let's all get in it.
> To Warsaw, for a holiday.

The Gestapo and the lusty *Rollkomando* Germans stood by. The children's singing merged with the wailing of the older ones as the procession of wagons moved away. Berele saw them go, his father, mother, his three sisters and poor battered little Simkhale in the doomed cavalcade. He turned from the window with a heavy heart and cried bitterly. Now there was only his old aunt to whom he could turn. Somehow she had escaped the rounding up and he went to her. For some days they lived in sorrow together but they were nearly starving. In the end they had to venture into the open fields to gather grass for their food. There were many others reduced to the same plight. But even this was eventually denied them. There was a roar of engines and the Gestapo hurtled up in their lorries. They stopped. Then another sound spat out. The Gestapo's machine-guns mowed down the starving, distraught people. Berele saw his aunt fall. It was another grim sight for his young, but no longer immature eyes. He lay pressed to the ground, his hands clutching the grass until his enemies went away.

Now he really had to plan where to hide. He thought of "Shishkowice." It was the place where the "big-shots" (*Shishkes*) lived. They were like the thorny berries that grew on the topmost branches of a certain tree and thus were they named. It was in the suburb Marishin. The Germans annexed this suburb to the Ghetto in order for the Jews to be able to get through to the cemetery. There was also the additional reason of having a direct rail-route to the death-camps. There was no train going through this district before the war. Now, during the *Sperre*, the victims were transported on the Marishin line. Here lived Rumkowski in his summer mansion, the officials, the commissars, the councillors and others whom Amtsleiter Hans Bübow (blast his name) had freed from the Resettlement. Here, too, were the orphanages and hospitals that had been liquidated and turned over to Bübow's favorites. The Jews called these favorites: "Bübow's children" and "Bübow's parents." There was food here and shelter of a sort.

Berele made his way there, climbed to the roof of one of the buildings and hid under a barrel.

At last the "*Aktion*" was ended and large posters proclaimed:

"SPERRE LIFTED. I ORDER ALL JEWS TO GO
TO WORK AND SPEED UP PRODUCTION FOR
THE TIME LOST!
                    AMTSLEITER HANS BÜBOW"

A few days later German newspapers carried pictures with captions: "Jewish mothers in the Ghetto of Lodz abandoning their children and the SS taking pity on these Jewish children."

Berele was free now but sad and lonely. He was as lonely as a rock. He thought of his father and mother; of how he used to play with his little brother; of how they used to share their bits of bread and the watery soup. Even those harsh days seemed kindly now. He was indeed alone. But many others were also afflicted. There was the woman whose two children had died of typhus and whose husband had been taken away by the Germans. She, too, was as lonely as a rock. And so it came about that she and Berele adopted one another. She lavished her love upon him and cherished him as her own. And he slowly and gratefully became accustomed to his new mother.

There still remained problems. Only children of twelve and over were allowed to work, and only those who worked were allowed to remain in the Ghetto. So nine-year-old Berele, no longer innocently young, was registered as thirteen years old. Thus ended the harrowing autumn, and winter came upon them.

Winter. In the Ghetto, frost is as bitter inside as out. No firewood could be found. The houses are wet both summer and winter. In summer the walls rot and fungi begin spreading. The dampness is rancid. In the winter, the walls, ceiling, and floors glisten with white snow. In every utensil, where there is a drop of water, it turns to ice. The windows are covered with a thick layer of ice and snow, as well as a dark blanket—as an air raid precaution—which is never removed because on leaving for work it is dark and on returning home from work it is also dark.

Berele must get up each day at five-thirty in the morning. He shivers from cold and never warms up. When one's hungry, one is cold. Ever since Berele has been in the Ghetto he has never had a full meal.

He would like to lie curled up a while longer under the

cover, but he must dress and be off to work. Dress? Because of the cold he sleeps with his clothes on. It would be silly to undress in this frost when it is as cold inside as out. While it is still dark, Berele lifts the heavy, wooden-soled shoes onto his feet, and putting on his coat, makes his way over the slippery, broken pavement, the clattering of his sabots sounding in the distance. With a pot hanging by a string around his neck, he hurries to work at the "Resort" (factory) together with tens of thousands of other Jews.

The wind flails Berele's body. The frost cuts his face and pricks the skin under his fingernails. A full moon and scattered stars shine down from a blue, darkening sky. The snow plays about under Berele's feet.

Clip-clap, echoes a rataplan of sabots. The tooting of a loco-motive and the clattering of coaches are heard coming in. One rooster crows—a second answers. Dogs are heard howling. This reminds Berele that not far off there is a world, a free life. A yearning for freedom gnaws at his heart, but he consoles himself with the thought that the war cannot, after all, last forever and soon he will be back with his parents.

Each step of Berele is accompanied with fear lest the Germans who stand guard by the barbed wire will, God forbid, decide to amuse themselves by shooting at him, as they so often do with the Jews.

Berele must be at the factory on time. Everyone must be at work at seven o'clock. He has a long distance to walk and if you're late, your punishment is—no soup. The soup consists of a few pieces of dried-up kohlrabi afloat in half an ounce of water (three-quarters of an ounce for children). Fresh kohlrabi is used as food for cattle, but when you cut up the kohlrabi and dry it out it becomes wood. This soup was the mainstay of daily life.

Berele worked in a children's garment factory. Only children worked there. One adult, the instructor, supervised the work. Up till the *Sperre*, this building had been a children's hospital. On the third anniversary of the war's outbreak, the Germans liquidated all the hospitals in the Ghetto of Lodz. The Gestapo came round in trucks, surrounded the buildings, and threw the patients (both the adults and children) out of the windows, like logs of wood. The more sturdy ones who tried to run away were shot on the spot. During the *Sperre,* the Germans turned these buildings into Gathering Points for the victims. Here, in the wards of the former children's hospital, stood two rows of machines. Each child sewed one part of a military uniform. Some children sewed by hand, some by machine, and others pressed.

The children turned out first-class work. They put their whole soul into it, turning out by the thousands uniforms for the German military. They had a special production quota to meet. They were responsible for each uniform, just like adults. The smallest defect was regarded by the Germans as sabotage. When a German commission came to inspect this children's garment factory they were dumbfounded at the productiveness of the Jewish children.

Berele was called "Klepsidre" (obituary), because he had the appearance of a skeleton. He could barely support himself on his thin legs and could just manage to move around.

When a German commission came to the factory, Berele hid himself because of his sickly appearance.

There was at one time a frightful famine in the Ghetto. Apart from the piece of synthetic bread and watery soup there was nothing else to be obtained. Like the adults, the children grew weaker and weaker, and they found it impossible to turn out the required quota.

The factory supervisor ordered the soup portions to be discontinued. The children argued: "If you take our soup away we will not be able to turn out the work."

The majority of the children belonged to the Underground Movement of all the united parties in the Ghetto.

Berele also took an active part in the Underground Movement. The children were told stories of heroes who sacrificed their lives for freedom. Also stories of the oppressed who fought for and achieved their freedom. The children were fired with the spirit of fighting for their rights. Berele's dream was to become a Judas Maccabeus.

Berele's parents had been socialists, so he knew how to organize a strike.

When the supervisor saw that the children were of one will, he decided to spread envy and hatred amongst them by distributing fifteen soup-coupons for more than one-hundred children. Berele jumped up on a bench, waving his coupon. With his weak voice and like a prophet, he roused and fired the hearts of the children.

"Friends: We must be as one with those who did not get any soup, for are we then any better than they? Do they not hunger as much as we? My advice is for no one to take any soup till everybody gets a portion. One for all, and all for one."

"Bravo. Bravo," the children cried out cheerfully.

When they brought pots of soup, not a single child went up, even though they were all frightfully hungry. Most of the children hadn't eaten since the day before.

The pots stood open and the steam drifted out from them. The taste of soup spread all over the room, teasing the stomach.

The soup distributors could not understand what had happened to the children. Every day there is a mad rush for the bit of soup, everyone wants to be first in line. Today—nobody moves, all are silent; no one wants his portion. They did not know that this was all Berele's work.

The factory manager immediately telephoned the "Kaiser" of the Ghetto, Mordecai Chaim Rumkowski, to let him know what was happening.

The "Lunatic" (that is what the Jews called him) rushed over in his cab.

The first thing he did was to castigate several boys, in order to instill fear into the children. The he jumped on one boy—with his left hand he held on to his eyeglasses and with his right he beat the boy, shouting at him with his Lithuanian-Jewish accent, "Shpeak, who are the unionishts?"

The youth answered nothing.

The blood rushed to the "Kaiser's" face. His brow wrinkled up and his silver, philosophic mane quivered. He went at a second boy, and at a third. He lashed and kicked with his officer's boots, yelling spasmodically: "Shpeak! Who are the unionishts? I'll kill you all!"

The children said nothing.

The "Kaiser" regained his breath, and then appealed to those children whom he had not beaten: "Tell me children, for you are the whole of my life (the "Governor's" favorite expression), who be those who won't let you eat the bit of soup?" With a fawning smile he looked each child in the eyes. No one answered him. The "Kaiser" became enraged and cried out: "Are you telling or not? If not, I'll have you all whipped!" (In the Ghetto they whipped people for the smallest transgression.)

The children remained silent.

"My children," he suddenly said fawningly and in a tone of voice one used when about to reveal a secret, "whoever tells me who the unionists are, I will give him a half-pound salami. Well, who'll be the first to tell?"

Such a gift was, in the Ghetto, like the requital granted to a condemned man who is already on his way to the gallows. With this offer he felt certain he had caught his prey. But he was disappointed. With great fury he picked out 10 boys: "You! You! You! Three days *fekalie* duty (to clean out with hand-scoops the toilets, and carry the barrels of refuse tied to one's back through all the streets of the Ghetto). And today you'll get the *plague* (another of his favorite expressions), not soup! Like dogs you'll lie here in the factory till nine at night! Not a speck of food will *I* allow to be brought to you! Only the *plague*!"

The children accepted the punishment in silence.

When the old man rode away, Berele started singing and all the children after him:

> Chaim, our Governor is a real fine guy,
> He'll have us eat yet rolls, butter and pie.
> Rumkowski Chaim pondering lay,
> Working hard by night and day,
> Made a Ghetto
> With a quota
> And insists—'tis the way.
> Rumkowski Chaim is Elder of the Jews,
> With the Gestapo he's quite chappy,
> Really feels as brother to us—
> And supplies us with some pappy...

ירחמיאל גרין

לאָמיר פֿאַרבלײַבן

אַזוי ווי דו ביסט נעכטן איז מיר,
לאָז פֿאַרבלײַבן מיר ליב:
אַזוי ווי דו ביסט נעכטן...

1940

Do Not Despair

It is but a passing wind—
Do not despair, my child
We are old trees, deep and broad,
Rooted in the earth,
With large crowns
That adorn the world.
Strong gusts
May tear the leaves from us,
May break our branches,
But not our crowns.
Strong deep-rooted trees
Cannot be torn out by the wind,
Nor can they be uprooted.
We are eternal trees
Giving nourishing fruit to the world.
We will be eternal!
It is but a passing wind—
Do not despair, my child.

Translated from the Yiddish
by Theodor Primack

AFTERWORD
My Father, Rachmil Bryks

BY BELLA BRYKS-KLEIN

We are familiar with the Holocaust survivor who under-standably wants only to forget his suffering and to blot out the painful memory of his Nazi nightmare, not even sharing it with his children.

There is also the Holocaust survivor who not only does not want to forget, but who cannot forget: he re-lives his traumatic experiences every single day for the rest of his life. This was my father, Rachmil Bryks.

He believed it was his holy mission to tell the world what the Nazis did to the Jews in the Holocaust, and that is the rea-son G-d let him survive. In each of his stories, there is hope, trust, that G-d did not forsake his people. He told me that he had written his books with tears and in agony, living through every separate torment of his characters. He wrote with simple words so that everyone would be able to understand. That is why his work, created in suffering and in pain, possesses such depth and strength.

My father was born April 18, 1912 in the small East European shtetl of Skarzysko-Kamienna, which lies between Radom and Kielz in Poland. He was the third of a family of four brothers and four sisters and was raised in an Orthodox Jewish home.

In his book *Di Vos Zaynen Nisht Gebliben* (*Those Who did Not Survive*), my father lovingly describes the town's characters, weaving these tales through the daily life and home of his wealthy uncle Mendel Feldman. This story allows us a glimpse into the almost forgotten world of the Polish Jewry, as well as the unique traditions and superstitions of that time. The Skarzysko ghetto was liquidated in October 1942, and all the townspeople including my father's family: his father Tevye, his mother Serl, his sister Esther with her husband Yechiel and their two children Moishele and Ruchele, his sister Tobtche with her husband Yidel and their child, his sister Leah with her husband—were taken to Treblinka and killed on Simkhat Torah in 1942. His brother Yitzchok was killed in Auschwitz in 1944. His brother Simkha served in the Polish Army and returned to Skarzysko-Kamienna after the war. Two days before his wedding, a Polish Nationalist shot him and his bride.

My father was not taken, since at the age of fourteen, he had left Skarzysko to help support his family by working as a hat-maker and a housepainter in the large industrial city Lodz. His artistic talents began to flourish here. He studied drama and performed in the Yiddish Theater of Lodz. In 1939, his book of lyric poems *Yung Grin Mai* (*Young Green May*) was published in Lodz to great critical acclaim.

From May 1940 until August 1944, my father was fenced inside the infamous Lodz Ghetto. In spite of indescribably difficult conditions, he began here to set forth his literary work. Here he wrote his ballad "Ghetto Fabrik 76" ("Ghetto Factory 76"), which was found buried after the war at the site of the ghetto. This describes the forced labor of the Jews in the chemical waste utilization plant. His original writings are in the archives of the Jewish Historical Institute in Warsaw, Poland. In later years, he wrote his "A Katz in Ghetto" ("A Cat in the Ghetto"), "Der Kaiser in Ghetto" ("The King of the Ghetto") and "Die Papirene Kroyn" ("The Paper Crown"), all of which give an in-depth portrait of Mordechai Chaim Rumkowski, the still-disputed Nazi-appointed Jewish ruler of the Lodz Ghetto.

The Lodz Ghetto was liquidated by the Germans, and in August 1944 my father was transported to the death camp, Auschwitz. Through the tragic story of one heroic family, he describes in his

"Oyf Kiddush Hashem" ("Kiddush HaShem") the unimaginably cruel behavior of the Nazis and their helpers. My father felt that writing about millions of people would weaken the tragedy. Isaac Bashevis- Singer wrote in 1953: "Every page of Bryks's book is Jewish history. If there had remained as detailed a chronicle of the destruction of the Temple as Bryks succeeded in recording, Jews would read it every Tisha BeAv and shed rivers of tears. It is a sacred duty to buy and read Bryks's book."

As all the handwritten manuscripts he brought with him from the Lodz ghetto were confiscated in Auschwitz, and possession of a pencil or a paper was strictly forbidden, my father, starving, after a hard day's work, lay on his filthy board, and recited all his works in his head.

Jews have always revered their folk writers; so too in the ghettos and concentration camps, the other inmates gave him pieces of bread from their meager rations. They who were about to die wanted to make sure that at least he survive the war so that he could write and tell the world what the Germans and their collaborators did to the Jewish people.

He was transferred to the Wattestadt camp, then Ravensbruck, and finally to Werbelin where the American Army liberated him on May 2, 1945. He was initially treated at Bergen-Belsen hospital; sick, weak and half-dead, the Red Cross brought him to Sweden for treatment. In spite of his suffering, while in the hospitals and sanitoria, he continued writing, and recited his poems before groups of Jewish refugees in Stockholm in order to encourage them.

At one such gathering, he met a young Transylvanian woman, Hinda Irene Wolf, a survivor of Auschwitz. They fell in love, and got married in the Great Synagogue on September 15, 1946. My sister Myriam Serla and I were both born in Stockholm.

From Sweden, my father carried on an extensive correspondence with Professor Max Weinreich of the YIVO (The Yiddish Research Institute) in New York, providing the prestigious institution with important documents of the Lodz Ghetto and of Scandinavian Jewry. With YIVO sponsorship and the aid of HIAS (the Hebrew Immigrant Aid Society), the family immigrated to the United States on the SS Stockholm on March 15, 1949.

From very early childhood, the Shoah was a part of our day to day life at home in New York. My parents freely discussed this period in front of my sister and me. Sometimes when my father would touch upon a particularly difficult episode, my mother would say, "Don't talk of this to the children; they are too young."

To that, my father would emphatically reply, "Nein! Zay musen vissen!" (No! They must know!").

We were always amazed by his phenomenal memory, by how he could recall minute details of the ghetto and the camps even twenty-five years later. In his stories, he painted the confined Jews' way of life, their mode of dress, their language, their mentality—like a living museum.

We were told of the brutality, of the cruelty of the Nazis and yet at the same time, my father instilled in us a sense of optimism: the resilience of the Jewish soul and the Jewish people. He reminded us that throughout Jewish history, a leader, an enemy, has arisen in every generation determined to destroy the Jewish people, but we always managed to overcome.

I vividly recall my father sitting in our sunny living room in the Upper West Side overlooking Broadway, using the dining room table as his desk, wearing a long-sleeved pressed white cotton button-down collared shirt with a sleeveless bordeaux wool vest, writing with his Parker fountain pen. My sister Myriam, five and a half, and I, Bayla, four years old, would be together in our room. When we raised our voices in play, my mother would rush into our room with her index finger on her lips, "Shhhh! Papa shreibt!" ("Hush! Father is writing!"). And we would continue playing very quietly.

When my father would finish a chapter, he would gather the family together, and would read the chapter in Yiddish to us and we would help think up titles for his stories.

We were permitted to speak only Yiddish at home and with my parents. It was most important to my father that his children be able to speak Yiddish.

My father used to sit with me in the evening, and, with a great deal of patience, teach me Yiddish from a little book of funny children's poems.

The Jews in the ghettos possessed no weapons to fight against the Nazis, but they proudly displayed spiritual resistance. In his article "The Corpus of Yiddish and Hebrew Literature from Ghettoes and Concentration Camps and its Relevance for Holocaust Studies," Prof. Yechiel Szeintuch of the Hebrew University of Jerusalem writes, "We must extend the concept of 'resistance' to apply not only to armed resistance, but also to spiritual resistance which preceded armed resistance during the years of Jewish persistence in living a Jewish life in the ghettoes and in the camps, a life of cultural activity and community organization, and self-help." Ongoing research in Israel is revealing a growing amount of documentation calling for a revision of the once-claimed passivity of the Jews "as sheep to the slaughter." Part of this spiritual resistance was the cultural life in the ghettos and the effort to preserve human dignity.

My father contributed articles to the Yiddish daily newspapers in New York City and enjoyed taking me along to the Lower East Side. Before catching the subway uptown, we always stopped at the Garden Cafeteria which was just around the corner from the presses. My father, over a hot glass of tea, would have a chat with whomever he chanced to meet there. I drank my hot chocolate at times sitting opposite such literary giants as Isaac Bashevis-Singer, Itzik Manger, B.Y. Bialostotzki, Shea Tennebaum, Lutzky, and Avrum Reisen.

My parents often took us to the Yiddish theater. We loved its drama and its comedy and enjoyed it tremendously since we understood every spoken word.

In spite of all they had suffered, my parents still had deep faith in G-d and instilled this in us. They taught us to help the less fortunate ones, and always give Tzeddaka (charity). It was also very important to them that we receive the best Jewish education available.

I attended Stern College—Yeshiva University, and in my junior year, I won a scholarship for a one-year study program at the Hebrew University of Jerusalem. I came to Israel in 1968, with the intention of completing my fourth year back in New York City at Stern. During that year though, I fell in love and in July 1969, married a wonderful person Yonah Klein, and I have been living in Israel ever since. I am presently doing my Master's degree in Yiddish Literature at the Hebrew Univ. of Jerusalem.

The last time I saw my father was in February, 1974. My husband and I flew from Israel to New York to show my parents our newborn daughter, Sarit. Eight months later, on the Sukkot holiday in October 1974, my father had a sudden stroke and died in his sleep, like a Tzaddik (righteous person). I was then pregnant with my second child, a son, who carries my father's name: Rami Rachmil.

My father died in New York City at the age of sixty-two. As my parents had planned Aliyah to Israel, my mother had his casket flown to Israel for burial on the Mount of Olives in Jerusalem.

On the first anniversary of his death, my mother published his "Di Antloifers" (The Fugitives") describing how the Germans invaded Poland and "Fun Gsise Zu Leben" ("From Death to Life"), detailing how he got out of Auschwitz.

Twenty-six years later, in 2000, on the eve of Rosh Hashana, my dear mother passed away in New York City and my sister and I brought her casket for burial next to my father on the Mount of Olives in Jerusalem.

My father had donated all his papers to the YIVO and these are contained in twenty-seven cartons in the YIVO archives. In the summer of 2004, I prepared a detailed inventory of my father's papers which include manuscripts, press clippings, personal documents, and correspondence including letters from Isaac Bashevis-Singer, Elie Weisel, the Lubavitcher Rabbi, and other personalities.

From the abyss of despair and desolation, after indescribable suffering, my parents, with enormous willpower, decided to marry and have children, to continue to a new world in order to build a spiritual home, full of love and devotion, tolerance and compassion. This is the ultimate triumph and strength of the human spirit.

I am very proud that we, as second-generation Holocaust survivors, have succeeded in passing on our beautiful heritage to our children. We are all proud Jews. In this way, I believe we are respecting and preserving the memory of the grandparents we never met.

When my father published his books in the 1950s and 1960s, it was too close to the actual war and readers were not yet ready to deal with the atrocities of the 1940's. My father died too early to realize the full impact of his writings. Today his works have become part of the teaching curricula in many Holocaust university courses throughout the United States and the world. His stories are being included in Holocaust anthologies and readers. His works have been translated into English, Hebrew, German, Italian, Swedish, and other languages. His "A Cat in the Ghetto" was dramatized by Shimon Wincelberg and was successfully performed by the Royal Swedish Theatre in Stockholm in 1970 and recently in Chicago. An opera was written by Bert Shaw. His poems were also set to music by William Gunther.

My father had been optimistic throughout the war years, but he told me more than once, that a Holocaust could happen again, and it is possible even in the U.S.A. He felt disappointed and disillusioned in the second half of the twentieth century when he realized that the world remained unchanged despite the genocide of World War II. It seemed to him that the nations had not learned anything.

People of the twenty-first century are trying to understand how enlightened human beings were able to systematically inflict such cruelty and suffering upon other humans.

Professor Frederick C. Grant, a Christian theologian, wrote in "The Churchman" that my father's books must be read in order "to awaken people to the dangers we are still in, as long as race hatred, segregation, isolationism, and unbridled sadism" exist.

My father devoted the last twenty-nine years of his life to commemorating the memory of the martyrs. He believed that if we let the world forget, there could be another Auschwitz.

I feel it is my moral duty to continue his holy mission.

Petah Tikva, Israel